DARK SUN

A Wicked Lovely Courts Book

MELISSA MARR

ALSO BY MELISSA MARR

Thriller

Pretty Broken Things (2020; psychological thriller)

Fantasy

Graveminder (HarperCollins, 2011)

The Arrivals (HarperCollins, 2012)

Cold Iron Heart (2020; *Wicked Lovely* adult)

The Wicked & The Dead (2020; Urban Fantasy)

The Kiss & The Killer (2021; Urban Fantasy)

Dark Sun (2021; Urban Fantasy)

Young Adult Fantasy

Wicked Lovely series (HarperCollins, 2007-2012)

Made For You (HarperCollins,, 2013)

Seven Black Diamonds (HarperCollins, 2015)

One Blood Ruby (HarperCollins, 2016)

Middle Grade Fantasy

The Hidden Dragon (Penguin, 2023)

The Hidden Knife (Penguin, 2021)

The Blackwell Pages trilogy (with Kelley Armstrong, Little Brown, 2012–2014)

Co-Edited with Kelley Armstrong (with HarperTeen)

Enthralled

Shards & Ashes

Co-Edited with Tim Pratt (with Little, Brown)

Rags & Bones

Dark Sun

By Melissa Marr

Previously in the series

At the end of the five primary Wicked Lovely books, the prequel *Cold Iron Heart,* or the various short stories (found almost entirely in *Wicked Mercy* or as standalones):

- Aislinn is the Summer Queen (*Wicked Lovely*) but no longer sharing the throne (as of *Darkest Mercy*) with Keenan.
- Donia, former Winter Girl, is (as of the end of *Wicked Lovely*) the Winter Queen.
- Keenan has left the Summer Court (in *Darkest Mercy*) and by the series end is the consort of Donia. In the epilogue to *Darkest Mercy*, Keenan uses the same staff that once cursed mortal girls

to try to be faery again. (This is explored in a short story in *Faerie Tales & Nightmares*.) For now, he's now bound to Donia as her consort, functionally the Winter King.

- Niall is the Dark King, which was his fate from before the primary five books. This took place at the end of *Ink Exchange*.
- Irial, former Dark King, died in *Radiant Shadows*, but he clung to his soulmate (Niall) and managed to become corporeal in *Darkest Mercy*. He is now the embodiment of Chaos.
- Leslie is finishing her four-year degree at the end of "Love Hurts" (including in both *Cold Iron Heart* and in *Wicked Mercy*). This sets the timeline for this book at four years after Darkest Mercy.
- . . . which means our young Summer Queen is 22-23 years old now.
- In the 1800s, Irial meets the first mortal he loved, Thelma Foy. They had two children: Elena Foy (Aislinn's grandmother) and Urian. Because Irial was afraid he had no self-control to let fate do as it must, he asked the High Queen (Sorcha) to curse him to forget Thelma.
- Sorcha, the High Queen, has hidden Urian from his father, Irial, for over a century. She sees the threads of fate, and so she is the behind-the-curtain manipulator to protect faeries, as well as the land of Faerie where she rules.

Now . . . you can read (or maybe did read!) any or all of those, but in case you haven't (or it's been a minute), I wanted to add this note to refresh your memory or bring you up to speed! I added a short story at the end for the same reason.

PROLOGUE: SORCHA

FOUR YEARS AFTER DARKEST MERCY
Prologue: Sorcha

Standing before the High Queen, Irial-- former Dark King and currently the embodiment of Chaos--looked somehow more regal in Faerie than he should. He held no dominion here, hadn't for centuries. He wasn't even Sorcha's balance now, but Irial was as commanding as he had been when he was ruling the creatures of nightmares. Faerie recognized it, or maybe Faerie merely reflected the High Queen's recognition.

Either way, the sky was cloudier, simply because Irial was *here* instead of in the mortal world where he lived. Once, he and all fey had lived in this world, removed from humans. Safe. Together.

But the once-Dark-King was a *gancanagh*, a seducer of mortals and faeries. Even Faerie was too small for him when he started feeling the urge to wander. Sometimes, the High

Queen had brought mortals here in hopes of forestalling his inevitable departure. Once, she'd even welcomed the first mortal he'd loved.

It had never been enough.

Irial was, in all ways, Sorcha's opposite. And though she still thought Irial *belonged* here, Sorcha had allowed actions to pass that resulted in closing the veil between Faerie and the world of mortals. There were exceptions, of course, to the closing of the veil. Some faeries could cross between worlds—just as in the beginning--but only a few exceptions traveled from here to the land of mortals.

Irial had always been an exception, and so was his son.

"I would say I regret that you had forgotten about your children," the High Queen explained. "But it was what was necessary to protect the threads of fate, and I have enjoyed Urian's company."

"You know him better than I do," Irial complained. "He's *my* son, and I've missed his whole li—"

"He's barely more than a century old, Irial. A teenager, as mortals call it." Sorcha smiled. "An angry boy child."

"When I was his age . . ." The former Dark King shuddered. "I was a monster."

"Do you say that you are no longer a monster? Ignoring rules. Asking favors. Believing you are an exception . . ." Sorcha said lightly.

Irial sighed. He might be almost as old as the first faery, but he was as much affect as impulse. Sorcha stifled a smile at his pout.

Gods save us, if he ever realizes I'm not as immune as he thinks.

Faerie was the domain of the fey, and their kind were all about exceptions. The entire reason behind rules was to break them. Some of the fey had forgotten that, but not

Irial. Never Irial. He'd defied death itself in order to stay with his beloved. He was a fool for love and had been for over a thousand years.

"Are you absolutely certain that you can't help me this time, love?" Irial asked the High Queen in that familiar wheedling tone. "What if you just bring Urian here to Faerie? Trap him. If you want, I could even move back, take up my old role opposite you, help with him, live within the boundaries of--"

"No." Sorcha frowned at him, seeing the future threads of violence that would follow if Irial tried to leave Niall.

"*Sorcha . . .*"

"I see all of the possible futures. So why would you presume to interfere without knowing the threads?" Sorcha prompted, both curious and irritated. "Do you not recall what your beloved Niall was like when he lost you?"

"He has Leslie. In time, they'd be fine without me." Irial paced like a caged monster. "And I *presume* because I have children, Sorch. A son. A daughter who raised her children to hate what I am. A son who wants my death. I had no idea that Thelma . . . that we . . . that I had *any* children. My son, who is apparently over one hundred years old, is furious about things which *I cannot fix*."

"The boy has a right to contest the throne," Sorcha repeated for the third time. "He has the right to contest both thrones. His mother's and his father's."

"Thelma never took the damn Summer throne. I hid her, and apparently impregnated her, so she was never the Summer Queen," Irial said, voice louder now.

He was no longer Sorcha's opposition, that role fell to the current Dark King—as much as to the Shadow King within Faerie itself. Since Irial hadn't been the Dark King this last blink of years, his temper was merely interesting, not a cause for concern.

Still, Sorcha crossed her arms.

Opposition *was* interesting, and Irial, for all his machinations, had always forgotten how to use any sort of logic when love entered the equation. His beloved Niall and Leslie were not likely to bring the Dark Court home to Faerie, and leaving Niall was how the courts had been drawn to war a blink ago, so Irial's proposed solution was impossible.

Sorcha's plan, however, had reasonable odds. She wasn't certain it would work, but she had faith in Urian.

The High Queen tugged several clouds from the sky and fashioned them into a pair of chairs and a table. Irial flopped into a chair, reshaping it with a remembered skill that he should no longer be able to utilize.

But he does. He acts as if he owns the world.

If only more of them would.

With more poise than she liked to have to use with him, the High Queen looked at Irial and repeated the same argument they'd been having since he'd learned of his children: "Thelma was the destined Summer Queen, and had you not hidden her away from Keenan and impregnated her, she *would* have been queen. Ergo the crown could have moved to Urian or to Elena."

"But Thelma *wasn't* the Summer Queen, so the throne isn't theirs." Irial kicked his feet out in front of him and pouted. He somehow managed to look like an indolent boy even after all these centuries.

Sorcha lowered her voice. "Do you think *I* forget, Irial? I saw you rescuing Thelma's granddaughter. Moira was destined to take the Summer throne, too. *Twice* you intervened. Twice the world risked death because of your meddling . . . and the world was in peril because *you* cursed the Summer Court. You are reaping the seeds you have sown, Irial."

He had become far too used to a life where he got what he wanted—or some facsimile thereof--but Sorcha believed in balance above all else. There had to be a balance for the things he'd stolen.

His debt was past due, and they both knew it.

Irial switched to attempted negotiation. "Could you at least help me mitigate—"

"No. I allowed your rescue of Thelma, however dangerous it was. She was able to have time with you. She gave you children. I allowed her to live here to let you know her and your eldest child." Sorcha couldn't understand his refusal to at least attempt to be logical. "*Children*, Irial. You have children."

"Children I didn't recall fathering until they were grown," he grumbled. "Had you ever planned to tell me?"

Sorcha laughed at his sullen expression. He was far happier these days, but a happier *gancanagh* was still a dangerous creature. And she saw threads of how wrong things could veer if he lost his happiness. Niall wasn't the only faery who needed the love the two men found with each other—and their increasing faery partner.

That's a truth for another day, though.

Sorcha reached out, uncharacteristically, and took his hand. "You demanded my vow that I would not tell you until Elena or Thelma sought you out. Would you have me believe the rules of our kind no longer apply to *me*?"

Sorcha pressed the matter, enjoying his flash of genuine fear. She had no desire to bring about the destruction that would follow if she entered the mortal world, but it was nice to terrify him.

"To bring Urian here would require that I walk there." Sorcha released Irial's hand. "I suppose I could meet your Leslie, and that absurd Summer Queen who refuses to visit here, and Winter . . . It has been a moment since I saw Keenan or the new Queen."

The former Dark King stared at her, silent now. She enjoyed his fear more than was strictly logical. Of all of their kind, she was the first—and since her twin's death--Sorcha was the *last* to embody pure faery magic.

As the first of her kind, she remade the world at a thought. Here, in Faerie, that was fine and normal. If she walked where the rest of her kind had fled, the human world, madness would consume their world.

So few humans remembered that magic was real.

So few humans saw their sort.

And so, Sorcha was bound to remain in Faerie, lest she release magic into the human world in ways that changed everything.

"The rules still matter," Irial allowed, his voice a whisper of defeat that disappointed the High Queen. A part of her felt toppled toward dangerous when *both* Irial and the Shadow Queen were here—and she liked it.

For a flicker of a moment, Sorcha wanted to help ease his worries, tell a pretty lie that everything would be fine, but the future was as of yet undetermined. The best she could say was, "Your son cannot be trapped in Faerie, Irial, and I cannot advise you on what steps to take. I cannot tell you where he is. I cannot even tell you what choices to make. The boy has a right to his grievances."

Irial took her hand. "As a friend and a parent yourself, can't you offer me anything?"

"He's *your* son, Irial. Maybe you ought to ask what *you* would do in his position."

The look of sheer alarm that met her hints was enough to make the High Queen sure that she had made the right choice. In his youth, the Dark King had no restraint, no awareness of long-term complications. He was id without conscience.

And his son was just as reckless so far.

Chapter One

KATHERINE

Katherine saw the faeries. Every day, she saw the fey walk past her as if she wasn't worth noticing. Strange, lovely shapes and forms that seemed to defy reason, legs too long and skins too thin. She was enchanted by their curious shapes: feathered, beaked, winged, and the most peculiar of all--those who looked nearly human. Sometimes they were ugly in a way that seemed to wrap right back to beauty. Teeth and talons, wings and whiskers, bones bared to the world, hands red with blood, there was no end to the variety in the invisible things she saw.

And not a one of them seemed to recognize her.

They had no idea that she shared half her blood with them, that she saw and heard them.

That was the goal, though. It was what her mother insisted she must do. Live a lie. Pretend. Act like she was just another human girl. Katherine could watch them from the safety of the window, as long as she avoided eye contact. She mustn't reveal herself. If she failed, they moved. It was that simple.

She'd failed quite a few times in her twenty-four years.

So far they'd lived in nine states before New Mexico. She remembered five of them: North Carolina, South Dakota, Florida, Pennsylvania, and Virginia. These days, the family was living in No Name, Somewhere in the Southwestern Desert. Somewhere, New Mexico.

Okay, technically, there was *probably* a name, but Katherine hadn't been inclined to bother learning it. Why bother when they were inevitably going to move again?

"Kit!" Her aunt stood in the doorway, not seeing, not knowing. Outside the window, something luminous slithered into the tree. Palo Verde tree. That name she did know. Literally, it meant "green tree" or "green stick." The tree itself was prettier than it sounded, especially right now when it was lit up by some fey thing glowing like it held the moon inside its body.

Katherine wanted to go out, to ask questions, to figure out where she fit. Instead, she turned her back to the faerie and smiled at her aunt.

Aunt Ida, of course, could not see the glowing thing in the tree. *She* didn't have the Sight. Most humans didn't.

"Yes, Aunt Ida?"

"You should not stay so late, twilight is not good for maidens," Aunt Ida said with the sort of tone that made quite clear that she was quoting something or other again.

Ida had been a librarian, an English teacher, a traveling musician, and any number of assorted jobs. For a while she worked making carnival masks and a few years back, she assisted a rock collector in the field. Being stationary was never something Aunt Ida did for very long, so tagging along with Katherine and her mother was easier for her than meandering alone.

I want to meander alone.

"I don't remember that one," Katherine admitted to her aunt.

"Rossetti, dear." Ida smiled and opened her mouth as if to continue.

"Right. Rossetti," Katherine said before her aunt could continue.

She couldn't love anyone more than she loved her aunt, but that didn't mean she was up for another rousing night of poetry recitation. Ida knew every bit of literature or song or film or art exhibit on the fey. Okay, maybe not *all* of them, but the significant or semi-accurate ones. Katherine thought Rossetti had somehow had more of a clue than the average mortal.

"I shouldn't linger in the 'glen' or take fruits from strangers. Got it," Katherine said.

The poem was a little too overt, especially with something fey outside the window. The last thing anyone wanted was to have a faery snatch Ida. She might romanticize them, and maybe Katherine did, too, but she remembered her father's warnings too: most fey things weren't like him. They were twisted in ways that made sadists look stable. At the best case, they'd leave you longing for something, *someone*, you couldn't keep--which was curable only if the faery in question died. If her father had left but were still alive, Katherine's mother would wither and die.

Of course, if he'd been so foolish as to try to leave them, Katherine was fairly certain her mother would've slid a long steel blade into his belly. Octavia Miller wasn't exactly a weak woman. It was more than a little intimidating to be her kid sometimes. Arguing with her was pointless. Outsmarting her was just about as likely as outfighting her.

Aunt Ida, however, was a curious mix of fluttering skirts and trailing scarves mixed with a liberal dash of willingness to get into the muck and mud. Mom was all muck, no flutter.

Katherine was still trying to figure out what *she* was.

Pulling her out of her thoughts, Ida said, "It's late, and it's just us tonight, so . . . can we close up?"

Dusk was not late by anyone's definition, but the euphemisms were necessary. They lived with the express goal of the fey never knowing who and what she was, that Katherine wasn't as human as her mother or aunt, that she could see them and hear them, that she was developing more and more traits that hinted at her father's lineage . . . it was frightening to Aunt Ida in a way that few things were.

On the other hand, it was exciting to Katherine—to be magical, to be *more* than a secret hidden in nameless towns across the nation. It was one of those things that made her wish time would hurry up a bit.

"I'll roll the shutters down tonight," Katherine offered.

It was a test, a sort of endurance game to see if she'd still be able to roll the steel blinds over the window. Steel, because of its iron component, was potentially deadly to the fey. As Katherine became increasingly fey, it stung to touch steel. Tonight, it hurt like she imagined touching a still hot kettle would hurt, not yet burning flesh but closer than comfortable.

Aunt Ida watched as Katherine steadied her expressions. She had to be able to fake being human.

Hiding the pain wasn't a lie, just an omission.

"Hands."

Reluctantly, Katherine held them out, palms up. "I'm fine."

Her aunt shook her head. "You can still lie to me. That's something."

The fey couldn't lie. Katherine's humanity was still intact, more or less, as long as she could lie. That was the working theory.

An inability to lie didn't sound terrible until a person started thinking about all the tiny lies that made up a day. When someone asks "how are you," most people lie. When friends ask, truth is easier, but in general, no one wants to answer that question with a *whole* truth. "What are you thinking" is another one. The thought of having to always answer that truthfully was enough for Katherine to wish to have her tongue removed.

"I try not to lie," Katherine offered. This, in general, was true, but the small lies, the little words that helped family not worry, were inevitable. "Touching the steel hurt, but it's not much worse than last month. You don't need to tell mom."

Ida stared at her, silent but obviously disbelieving. "Octavia will be home in three more days. I'll give you till then, but you know we have to tell her."

Her mother was wonderful in a lot of ways, a good mom. Devoted. Fun. She was also all about rules. No speaking to faeries. No exposing her true nature to faeries. Definitely no wandering off with faeries. She'd taught self-defense, both physical and mental, to Katherine since childhood. Swords. Guns. Herbs. Manipulation. If there was a tactic that she thought would protect her daughter, they pursued it. The result was that Octavia Miller was something of a bad-ass in the way that made Katherine feel inept.

"It's kind of you to give me the time," Katherine said,

reverting to the childhood lesson that the words "thank you" were empty and insufficient.

She looked at the steel shutter that was now sealing the world outside, preventing them from seeing in and her from seeing out. It wasn't uncommon in their neighborhood. Plenty of shops used them. Most homes had window bars. Most shops had the roll-down steel outside the glass. Her apartment had bars outside and roll-downs inside--mostly because her mother purchased them and mounted them in each rental unit they had as they moved across the country.

"You're changing," Aunt Ida said, admitting what no one else wanted to say. "They'll find you. Find us. Once you're less like your mother . . ."

And there it was--the thing that made Katherine lie awake at night, the detail that somehow both terrified and excited her. She didn't want the fey folk to find her family, but sometimes, when she let herself think of it, she wanted them to find *her.* Katherine remembered her father to a degree, but she didn't know another single faery.

What if he had other children? Were there siblings out there?

She knew that faeries like him--*gancanaghs*—were promiscuous. He'd been with fey and humans, more humans than he should've considering that he was literally addictive to them. She wasn't sure if she was addictive, too. If Katherine was, that meant she could never *ever* have a human boyfriend. So, her choices were to be single for her entire life or find a faery who didn't mind that she was part human . . . assuming she wasn't taken prisoner or killed for being half-fey.

Her father swore that the eldest of the faery queens kidnapped and imprisoned halflings like Katherine. Crossing the oldest faery queen sounded awful, but so did crossing *any* faery queen--the others he'd spoken of sounded wretched awful, too.

So single forever, that was to be her fate.

It could work. Really. It wasn't like she had any interest in being loved or . . . ugh. She couldn't even lie in her own head. Katherine was half-in-love with the mere idea of being loved, of being kissed, but she wasn't horrible enough to kiss some defenseless human boy or girl to find out if she was addictive to humans.

That left captivity or death.

Sometimes she hated her father, who had been entirely selfish enough to kiss human after human.

Chapter Two

AISLINN

Although the Summer Queen was not exactly expecting the appearance of her halfling uncle, she knew who Urian was when he strolled into her court. Shadows danced across the floor, as if they wanted to get closer, to touch, to meld with him. And had she been as insecure as she was when she took the throne of the Summer Court, Aislinn might have trembled at the anger in his every step and breath.

Instead, Aislinn found herself studying the stranger. She wouldn't have needed her great-grandfather's warning that the older faery was angry or the knowledge of a surprise relative to recognize Urian. He *looked* like family in some intangible way. Shadow-dark skin and what would've been a twin to her own dark hair before sunlight changed her.

"What shall I call you?" Urian didn't even lower his gaze, despite standing before a queen.

Aislinn waited.

"Niece?"

She smiled but said nothing.

"Ash girl?"

The Summer Court guards eased closer, and at that moment, Ash felt a flicker of fear. Urian grinned at their approach, even as he stood with his father's arrogance, unbowed and bold. Some of the same wicked glint that Irial often had glimmered in his gaze.

Briefly, she wondered if this is what Irial had been like before he'd found love. If so, it was no wonder that the former Dark King was so feared—or perhaps, this was what he was like when he'd lost his love? Either way, there was a tempering strength in love, a power that eased the edges of darkness.

Urian had nothing to ease the edges of the rage that seemed to animate him, and it made her fear him a little more. Aislinn lifted a hand to stop the guards who started to move closer.

"Murderess?" Urian whispered the word.

"Queen," Aislinn said louder.

"Not *my* queen." Urian glared at her. "I will never bow to you."

Aislinn repressed a shiver of fear. She was strong enough to fight any other faery in existence now—at least those who lived in her world. The first faery, Sorcha, was still a threat. But strong enough didn't mean that Aislinn wanted to fight anyone.

As if oblivious to the tension, Urian looked around. He paused and smiled at Siobhan; he winked at another guard.

"Why are you here?" Aislinn asked when he simply stood there as if this was a casual visit.

"I thought I should meet the child who cost Moira her life." Urian tilted his head before adding, "Pretty little murderess."

"I did *not* kill my mother," Aislinn started.

Urian brushed his hand to the side, and shadows slid across the ground as if he was summoning them. He shouldn't be able to manage that. The Dark Court belonged to Niall, and before that it was Irial's domain. It was *never* the right of this faery. The abyss-guardian-- the semi-sentient shadows that the Dark King had as shield, guards, and extensions of his will--were not a typical gift.

"No." Aislinn said only the one word, but it was enough. Sunlight flooded the room, chasing shadows away even as more of the Summer Court guards surged into the room, a rush of vine and bark and worry.

Urian smiled, cold and vicious. "Frightened?"

His was a look Aislinn had seen on the face of Bananach, madness tinged with fury.

"We are *fine*," Aislinn told her guards, motioning for them to leave.

Only Tavish and Siobhan stayed. It was enough. If they were anyone else in the court, Aislinn would feel unprotected, but Tavish was fierce and Siobhan was brutal when provoked.

"If you must address me, you may call me Aislinn."

"Aislinn," Urian echoed. "My sister's granddaughter. The last ashes of my family."

"Such an odd little mortal-turned-faery. You took my mother's crown, my niece's crown." Urian reminded her of the fey things that had been the stuff of nightmares for her growing up, vicious in ways she would never understand.

"Thelma didn't want this crown," she reminded him. "My mother didn't either."

"And you?"

"This wasn't the life I wanted, but it's *mine* now. This

court is *mine*." Aislinn felt her body glow brighter as her skin filled with sunlight bright enough that any faery not of her own court should wince and withdraw.

He didn't.

Urian laughed. "What makes you so interesting, Ashes? Friend to Dark, embodiment of the Summer, playmate of the son of the High Queen. Why do they care about you?"

"I don't know, Uncle. Why are *you* here?"

As Urian laughed this time, shadows skittered closer in defiance of her sunlight. Rage and hunger simmered in him, so hot that she could have been looking into Bananach's eyes.

Without meaning to, a sword of sunlight formed in Aislinn's grip, blinding bright and sizzling with heat.

Urian glanced at the sunlit blade. A smile identical to his father's curved his lips. "Do let them *all* know that I've come calling, Ashes."

Then he flung something glittering toward Siobhan.

"Siobhan!" Aislinn was halfway across the room before she finished the word, but Tavish was closer and almost as fast. He pushed Siobhan aside.

The blade that had been hurled at Siobhan stabbed Tavish's stomach. And then he was on the ground, blood pouring from his wound.

Her advisor. Her friend. Her brother-by-choice.

Aislinn was livid. The sword that was in her hand a moment ago was there and raised. She met her uncle's eye and stalked toward him.

"Will you let *him* die, too?" Urian asked, taunting her with the sort of voice best suited for playground quarrels. "Or will you kill the son of the last Dark King? Whose life matters to you? What do you choose today? Death or life, Ashes?"

Her guards came in again, spilling into the room like grains of sand caught in an angry tide, and her rage that she'd dismissed them was entirely directed at herself as Urian walked to the door and left as quietly as he'd arrived.

Chapter Three

URIAN

He'd expected more of a reaction—and not just from his niece. She was a child compared to him, barely old enough to be an adult as a faery. For a mortal, though, she was equivalent to a person only slightly younger than him. That was one of the oddities of being caught in a space between mortal and fey. Age was extremely relative.

Urian was well under two centuries or so. Adult for a faery, but not exactly *old* like his father or the current Dark King. Aislinn, because she'd aged as a mortal, was almost his equivalent age.

Of course, faeries born of *two* fey parents thought little of age. Eternity changed thinking in ways that were hard to comprehend at times. It was hell on ethics, as well.

He strolled out the door of the home of the Summer Queen just as a wave of sunlight started to glow. Then he made his way through the wretched town of Huntsdale with a speed that he'd practiced incessantly in his childhood. His tutor, his auntie, had taught him things that most faeries never knew. As he became a man, he'd realized why: she knew he'd go after his father one day, and she was preparing him.

When he came to the gate to Faerie, he parted the veil and stepped into the place of many of his happiest memories. The veil between Faerie and this world was locked. Urian had no idea why his aunt insisted on maintaining that closure. The war between the courts had passed, and his aunt had no logical reason to insist on that continuation. There were those who had a key, though.

Seth--the consort of the Summer Queen--was able to visit Faerie. In fact, Seth was a son-by-choice of the High Queen. And of course, the monster who was Urian's father could come and go freely. Irial was almost as old as Sorcha, and for centuries, he'd been her balance. He was the Dark King for centuries upon centuries. The High Queen's affection for him was the reason Urian's mortal mother had been able to live here.

But neither Seth nor Irial had the same access that Urian did. There were no rules, no protocol, no exceptions where he was concerned. He was a child of the High Court; as a boy, these strange spaces had been his home. He'd lived there for several decades, and he was ever-welcomed in Faerie.

Tonight, Urian opened the air to his side and stepped into the land of the fey.

He walked without pause to the gardens where he'd played as a child. And there, awaiting him as she always was, stood his aunt. Sorcha. The High Queen.

"Child." Sorcha opened her arms for an embrace. She looked far from the millennia-old creature she was, but she was one of the first faeries, born into a world that was of her own making.

Today, she looked merely mortal. Her hair was in some complicated upsweep; fire-red curls cascaded like waterfalls to her hips. And she wore a pair of jeans and a loose pale green blouse. Her feet were, as always, bare.

"Auntie." Urian swept her up in a hug that lifted her into the air for the express purpose of hearing her laugh. As a boy, he'd always found her tendency to swing him into the air joyous, and as a man, he wondered if she'd once done so to hear his laughter.

"Ask me no questions," Sorcha whispered as he lowered her back to her feet.

Urian stepped back, ignoring her words. "No dragon today?"

Sorcha laughed again. "I pondered it. So much more comfortable to avoid speech if I am shaped that way. Dragons are not much for words."

"You *are* the loveliest dragon in the world," Urian assured her.

But the High Queen wasn't easily charmed. "I am the *only* dragon since your father left—"

"No," Urian cut her off. "No tales of what he was like when the world was new. No tales of the magic that loved me."

"He did. He might not have met you, but he loved you even before he knew you existed. He used to watch your sister and your mother as if the world was nothing more than the frame around them." Sorcha smiled, not at Urian but at the memory of his besotted father.

Urian had seen that look often enough that he hated his father even more. She clearly cared for Irial—but Urian was too selfish to want to share Sorcha's affection, so he never remarked on it. Perhaps he ought to feel guilty, but Urian wanted possession of the love the queen had held for his father.

He considered trying to seduce either the current Dark King or the mortal that functioned as the Dark Queen for the two men who controlled the Dark Court. The cold truth was that Urian wanted to steal everything his father had.

"You know his supposed love matters not at all," Urian argued to the High Queen, reverting to a more stilted speech in her presence. "That man killed my mother."

"He loved her." Sorcha stepped closer and rested her hand on Urian's arm.

Urian, well-used to his aunt's ways, lifted his arm and offered her his elbow. "Maybe. He also killed her."

"Mortals die. All of them." Sorcha began to walk. The ancient faery had developed the habit of strolling through gardens that came into existence as they walked. And Urian realized as a boy—admittedly because his mother told him— that Sorcha had taken to telling him secrets by way of the worlds she built as they walked.

On rare occasions, the shapes of people walked in the shadows around them—stories or memories or threads of future-seeing that took shape to tell him secrets she wasn't able to capture in words.

"Have you seen anyone of interest?" Urian prompted.

Sorcha favored him with a sly smile before saying, "None so interesting as you, Child."

"Somehow I doubt *that*, Auntie." Urian shook his head.

"None so interesting to *me* as you are right now," she amended. "I understand that you threatened the Sunlight and the Dark."

He squirmed. "The usurpers have thrones that should be mine."

"Thelma would have shed tears that you are cruel to Aislinn *or* your father," Sorcha pointed out. She was, eternally, blunt to the point of pain, and in his earliest memories he saw his mother sitting at the High Queen's side.

"You ought to be intimidated," Sorcha chastised his mother, Thelma.

Thelma continued sorting through a pile of stones that the High Queen had either created or ordered gathered. As a boy, Urian had no idea how terrifying the High Queen was to most faeries. His mother treated her like a dear friend.

"Psh." His mother had given the queen a look that had quelled Urian more than a few times. "You aren't scary, Sorcha."

"I think you are, Auntie," a very tiny Urian had insisted, hoping to appease her with his words.

Sorcha looked at him. "You never have things to fear from me, Child. I would be the dragon to slay monsters at your side."

"His father is not *a monster." Thelma leveled a hard look at both of them. "The Summer King, on the other hand . . ."*

"It is a rare woman who defends the Dark," Sorcha had murmured. "Remember that, Child. Rare gems are harder to locate in that world, but they do exist."

Urian tore his gaze away from his memory, heart aching at the sight of his deceased mother.

"She changed everything." Sorcha glanced at a field that quickly shifted into a copse of trees. "His heart had been broken. Shattered by his own mistakes. His lover had left him, and then he met your mother."

"And broke *her* heart."

Within the shelter of those trees, Urian's mother appeared again.

"How can you love me?" Irial asked.

Thelma laughed and kissed him.

"I won't even remember you." He bowed his head and pulled her into a tight embrace.

"You taught me love, made me a mother, and gave me a safe home." Thelma tilted her head to look up at the Dark King. "I shall live in hope that you will remember me."

"Sorcha says you can come here whenever you need . . . if the baby had been a boy, you could stay." Irial looked away, swallowing hard. "I hate the thought of our daughter or her daughter marrying Keenan."

"I'll raise Elena to be wary. And she'll raise her child that way." Thelma sighed. "I feel guilty, too. I avoided it, but hadn't thought it would . . . that our child . . ." She started weeping then. "I don't regret it, though. I don't regret you. You taught me love."

Urian turned his back. Sometimes he hated that the High Queen shared these glimpses that were not *his* memories. He had never seen his parents that way. All he knew was that love of his father had cost his mother her life. She was mortal, in love with a *gancanagh*. That was why she died, no matter what anyone else thought. Urian was sure of it.

"Maybe she wouldn't have loved the Summer King, but she'd be alive still . . . and I wouldn't be"—he gestured at himself—"a monster too. And Moira wouldn't have died."

Sorcha sighed. "That's not how the threads work. If she hadn't fallen in love with Irial, the then Winter Queen would've killed her. Beira set out to have Moira die. She set out to murder Aislinn. . . and you, my small wonder, would have never existed."

Urian ignored the "small wonder" remark. He towered over the High Queen. "I would rather my non-existence than her death."

Sorcha stepped in front of him. "Obstinate child. She died no matter the path. Helping your father save your mother created more years for her, healed his heart, and thwarted Beira. Do not question my wisdom, Urian. I adore you, but I am still responsible for a great many things more than your wounded heart."

Urian bowed his head. She was the closest thing to true family he had. His relationship with his sister caused him too much pain, and both his mother and niece had died.

That left the monster who sired him and the usurper to his mother's throne. And the High Queen, who was not true family by blood. She was his by choice, though, and when so very many things were outside of choices, that made the ones he *did* have matter all the more.

He dropped to his knees. "I beg forgiveness, Auntie. I do not mean to doubt your wisdom. I love you."

"Remember that later when your own heart feels shattered," she whispered. "*He* was always destined to find love with a mortal. It is what his kind does. It is what he was fated to do." She paused and offered a sad smile. "It is what *your* kind does. Mortals or other *gancanaghs*. There is no other choice for you."

Urian stared up at her, mouth open, but he could only manage a single word: "What?"

Sorcha stepped back and slid into the shape of a dragon, which was the same as saying "I'm done with words and answers." Iridescent scales the size of platters covered a body that was massive and muscled. Spines that looked like triangular plates jutted up from her skull like a purple mohawk. Daintily, she tossed her head toward her back, directing him.

"I haven't ridden in—"

"Grrrr," the High Queen, currently reptilian in shape, answered.

"As you wish," Urian whispered.

And with more than a shade of trepidation, Urian stepped onto her outstretched clawed hand and braced himself as she dumped him on her back. He hadn't expected to fit as well as he had as a child, but magic adjusted for things in ways that weren't always logical—even when that magic belonged to the embodiment of logic.

As the High Queen's immense wings began to flap and they took flight, he was smiling in a way that he hadn't done in far, far too long.

Chapter Four

URIAN

Later, as he readied himself to leave Faerie, Urian pondered briefly that he'd left the building where the Summer Court lived without any injuries or issues. He wasn't going to admit that he was impressed that Aislinn had chosen to save the fallen fey rather than attack Urian to exact vengeance. He suspected that he'd have chosen differently.

There was no one—other than the High Queen and his sister Elena —he'd cared for enough to choose to help them. Not since his mother had died. Not since he'd realized what he was.

A drug.

There were nicer words, but the reality of life as a halfling was that the faery world would be deadly to him unless he established himself as a threat—and his time with humanity was dangerous in other ways. His touch was poisonous. And like any poison, he'd eventually kill.

Had killed, he mentally corrected himself.

When he was unaware of what he was, of the heritage dear old dad had left him, he'd accidentally killed a girl. They were at a party--kissing, touching--and a few weeks later, she started to wither. No doctor knew why she died. Urian hadn't known either. Then. After a few more deaths, and he'd noticed the pattern: His kisses were fatal.

But what life was there, then, spent around mortals? What future was there when one lived for literal centuries? He needed to be accepted within the world of the fey, but the more he'd considered it the more he realized that *acceptance* wasn't enough.

His father *owed* him.

His sister, Elena Foy, had not been cursed with this poisonous skin. Her only faery heritage was that she aged more slowly than mortals, and of course, she could see them. She'd raised her daughter—Urian's niece, Moira—and then her granddaughter, the current Summer Queen. They were all more mortal than fey, despite the blood running in their veins.

Urian was unusual in that he was more fae than mortal. He'd aged even more slowly, and his sister, though only a year older than him in physical years, was a grandmother while Urian was still the emotional equivalent of a twenty-something year old mortal.

Iron didn't injure him as it did most fey—but that was because he was destined to a king. It was his first inclination of the destiny that awaited him. Admittedly, halflings were always peculiar creatures, sometimes more fey and sometimes more mortal. Urian was almost entirely fey. In his look. In his traits. He was everything his father was, and he hated himself for it far too often.

Hated Irial for it.

So Urian had stayed hidden. He'd been living a life of gloved hands and celibacy for years at a time. The occasional halfling, often unbeknownst to themselves, or solitary faery was his only opportunity for the one thing he craved above almost all others: affection, touch, hunger.

He deserved more—and knowing that his damnable father was happy with some other mortal *and* a faery too? That was like vinegar in Urian's mouth that he couldn't escape. Urian's mother died waiting for Irial. Urian was left unable to find what he needed—what most faeries and mortals craved—thanks to this cursed heritage.

Shouldn't he have something to ease his losses?

Shouldn't he be happy?

He stepped back into the mortal world. "Why should *I* hide in the shadows? Blood of two courts. Abandoned by both."

Urian waited for the wild creature that shaped itself into a car as it approached. His car-friend-creature rarely ventured far into Faerie, but the creature was there, waiting as ever, when he stepped back into the mortal world. The creature, his only lifelong friend, carried him into the dark night. The car didn't speak, but the currently car-shaped creature was his companion, the one he spoke to freely and without fear of retribution.

The car drove, and eventually Urian let himself sleep. The distance to the desert where he was living was four days —unless he dropped into Faerie and then back out on the other side as he had done.

His auntie, as the eldest living faery called herself, allowed him unfettered access to Faerie although the veil was technically closed. Urian was grateful for the exception that his auntie had allowed him.

She must see that I am destined for greatness! Why else would she treat me this way?

He was smiling as he drifted to sleep in the bedlike seat that his creature offered for him.

When Urian woke, his car-that-was-not-a-machine had brought him to the edge of the openness that was New Mexico. Urian wasn't sure if the creature woke him or not, but he enjoyed the sights of the land as they zipped toward his home.

Few places could match it for its odd beauty—and he has certainly looked. Some places matched one's soul; of this, he was sure. Urian had stood at the edge of the ocean, peering into waters filled with strange and lovely creatures, flashes of darting color and shimmering scale. He'd stood atop mountains, fleet hooves and tufted furs. He'd meandered through tall grass prairies, where fleeing hares and buzzing insects were barely noticeable over the song of swaying grass. The world was lovely.

And yet no place had filled his heart the way the landscape of New Mexico did. The moon seemed somehow larger, as if it were a glowing ball of light that could slide into a sliver in the craggy earth. And the landscape was a mix of open spaces that made him feel freer and rugged insistence on survival against odds. It wasn't as hot as neighboring Arizona, or as snow-draped in winters as northern neighbor Colorado. It was a liminal space, a mix of many things.

Like me.

And maybe that was all *home* was-- a place that matched the shape of your soul. If so, New Mexico was the first home he'd found outside of Faerie. That meant, on some secret part of Urian's heart, that he'd expected to find peace here.

The land was everything he wanted, so shouldn't the urge to roam be quelled?

It wasn't, though, and so he thought that he'd hunt down his niece or his father. Perhaps violence was the answer?

He watched the moonlight across the sky, lighting trees and ravines. He waited as the car slid through mountainous sections, for New Mexico was not all desert. And with each minute and mile, he felt less lost. Not satisfied, but no longer fighting an urge to flee.

Home.

Then finally, the car stopped at a tiny house that could have been carved of stone. It was adobe: bricks made of heavy clay earth. And those bricks were built around a wooden frame. While Urian didn't suffer from the reaction to iron or steel that most fey things did—*thank you, mother*— he still preferred the naturalness of his stone home.

As he exited the car, it shifted until it looked like a mustang. Muscled, wild, and not meant for being trapped in a stable or garage. In the summer months, that would change. The desert sun was draining, but right now, the car-horse-creature was nickering and stomping.

"Go on," he whispered.

The horse-shaped faery creature brushed a sort of embrace against him, rubbing a softly furred face against his cheek, and then she was gone.

Urian stood watching the flurry of dust as the horse ran faster than any horse born in this world. Someday, he hoped that the creature would share her name, but for now, all he could say was, "Be well, my friend."

Because she was his only long-term friend, despite their being unable to speak in the same language.

Chapter Five

AISLINN

"Sunlight?" Tavish asked. It was a simple request, but her advisor knew what he was asking. Only the regent could heal with the element or aspect of the court, and if any faery was not true to the court, they'd die of it.

Are you sure? She stared at him, knowing he understood her hesitation.

Aislinn knelt at his side. "There are complications."

"I know," Tavish assured her, voice shaky from obvious pain. "The side effects . . . are acceptable. Appealing, even."

The Summer Queen said nothing. If she was wrong about his loyalty, if he was wrong about his nature, pressing sunlight into that would kill him.

If I don't try, he'll bleed out.

Aislinn found the gaze of her second advisor, who was rather desperately in love with Tavish, and told her, "You will escort Tavish to his room as soon as I fix this."

Aislinn nodded at the oozing wound. The edges were blackening as if ink had poured there, and the skin started to writhe. Siobhan swallowed as she stared at the wound. Memories of the war between the courts were still too fresh.

"Poisoned," Tavish whispered. "If you could heal me soon . . ."

Aislinn pressed her lips together tightly, as she lifted his torn clothing so that the bloodied skin was visible.

"Are you sure?" Aislinn asked. "We can call a healer and—"

He looked at Siobhan as he answered Aislinn. "Yes."

Aislinn nodded. "That yes was to you, Siobhan. Remember that."

Then, the Summer Queen pulled the sunlight into her hands. It felt like hot honey, too hot for anyone else to touch.

She knew she'd started to glow. Sunlight radiated from her entire body, as if she had summoned the sun itself and somehow held it inside her. The guards, the freed Summer Guards, and assorted Summer Court faeries all started flowing into the room as if they were being called to their queen's side.

They were more used to sunlit healing than she was, but there was an instinct guiding her. Once she'd healed the Summer King this way, but then she hadn't realized how sensual it would feel, how much need it would evoke in the person who was healed—or in the court. Raw sunlight was heady stuff, intoxicating in ways that made the strongest liquors seem mild.

"Be well, brother, and be loved," Aislinn whispered, and then she brought her hands down on the wound, cupped them there at first, and then pressed down.

Tavish moaned, first in pain as she seared whatever

poison had entered his body and then in a sort of agony as the skin sizzled and burnt.

When the Summer Queen finally lifted her hand, a tattoo was there, a sun much like the blackened sun already on Tavish's throat. Briefly, Aislinn realize that the other tattoo was likely from this same thing.

"My queen," Tavish whispered in the sort of awe that should be saved for divinity, but then he looked at Siobhan and murmured, "My beloved."

"Ash?" Siobhan prompted

"He's drunk on sunlight." Aislinn realized that she didn't sound much more sober. The room was erupting in flowers, and couples—or couples for the night—were already kissing and caressing.

Tavish slid his hand over Siobhan's leg, at first caressing her calf but within moments his hand was above the knee and showing no sign of stopping.

Siobhan caught his hand in hers and asked, "What are you doing?"

"Seducing you . . . ?" Tavish smiled drunkenly.

Siobhan stifled her giggle, and Aislinn turned away. There was still a wide swath of mortal awkwardness in her, and even though she learned to hide it, voyeurism made her feel incredibly awkward. And it highlighted that she far more monogamous than was typical of the court of sunlight. The last regent, the Summer King, had dozens of bedmates and was adding to them for centuries. Aislinn, however, was still mortal enough in her heart—despite being wholly fey in all ways--to want a happily ever after with one person.

And that one person was—

"Miss me?"

The Summer Queen turned to face the man who had appeared behind her. "Seth! You're to be in Faerie! How--"

"Sorcha said you would need me, and I thought—"

"My uncle was here to murder someone," Aislinn said, sounding far too light-hearted and knowing that it was the sunlight washing away her rage and fear. If she wasn't dizzy on sunlight, Aislinn might point out that she no longer *expected* him to be here when she needed him. He was always away, always busy, and she was lonely. She tried to chase those feelings, but her half-mortal lover stared at her with a smile that was proof that he was not resisting the crash of Summer energy that had filled her home.

Why not give in?

Seeing Seth still took her breath away. Several years in his arms and longer still of his friendship, and she still felt like the world tilted when he looked at her. Not quite mortal, not quite faery, he'd retained the tattoos and piercings that ought to feel toxic now that he was cursed to be fey. His just-this-side of razor-sharp cheeks looked inhuman to her now, but they'd been that way when he was mortal.

"Ash?"

"You're gorgeous," she breathed. "Like something that could be feral if the world tilted."

To the left someone moaned.

"Says sunlight given form," Seth murmured. "Should we address the murder attempt?"

Elsewhere were giggles.

The queen did not look. Instead, she pulled Seth closer. "Yes, but . . . can we talk about that later . . . I have more pressing needs I'd like you to address."

———

The next morning, Aislinn was propped up in the nest-like bed she'd created at some point. She looked at Seth, remnants of vines still wrapped around his wrists, and for a flicker of a moment, she wondered if she should feel embarrassed. Summer was a time of impulse, of longing and laughter. In ways, it was not so different from the Dark Court.

Without the pain.

And yet, there were vines wrapped around the arms of her beloved.

"I can hear you worrying," Seth murmured, opening his eyes to look up at her. "I had fun, Ash."

"You have bruises, Seth."

"I'm fey enough to withstand a drunken Summer Queen these days," he reminded her, more edge in his voice than either of them likely wanted.

"I just. . . that wasn't something we discussed and—"

"*Summer* Queen. Granddaughter of the last Dark King." Seth shrugged, looking as calm as usual. "Don't like *him* still, but I do tolerate him for Niall. They get up to things that make these bruises look like--"

"Comparing me to them? Not really helpful." She crossed her arms.

"Hey?" he said softly.

Aislinn glanced at him, feeling awkward that her tears were creating a small rainfall in the room. Again.

"I had *fun*." Seth stressed each word. "I wouldn't change a thing, but if you're interested, maybe next time you use those vines in a way that leaves you at *my* mercy."

Aislinn took a deep breath, picturing that in far too much detail. He always knew how to distract her. "Now? Now could be—"

"Ash?" A voice called through the bower of flowering vines. "The Dark Court is here. Are you--"

"Coming!" she called out.

Seth gave her a laughing look, but instead of a predictable teasing retort said, "Low hanging fruit, Ash. I'm not going there."

"Really? I like you there." Aislinn smirked and in a blink, vines extended from the remaining pieces on his wrists to the edges of the bed. "We'll discuss it later."

"Ash . . ."

She kissed him until he was strained on the restraints for a different reason. Then she looked down at her consort, her beloved, her best friend, and smiled. "Be back in a while."

"Ash . . ." Seth twisted against the new restraints. "Seriously?"

She was still giggling when she left the room, especially because those vines would vanish in about two more minutes. She would never hurt Seth on purpose—or trap him. That didn't mean she was above teasing him.

Sometimes it was good to be queen.

Chapter Six

KATHERINE

Stealing was wrong. In fact, Katherine was certain that it was on the list of rules she kept in her room, probably top ten even, but it didn't *feel* wrong. Causing Aunt Ida stress? That was wrong. Worry her mother? Wrong. Going outside for a drive? That didn't *feel* very wrong--even though stealing the keys was required for her to do so.

It wasn't like she was off chatting with faeries though. For her, "wrong" was relative to the fey. All questions came back to the fey.

In the giant exercise studio that was why her mom picked this house, Aunt Ida was meditating to some gong and drum cacophony that she thought was "soothing." It was making Katherine feel anxious. The weather was nice, and Katherine had a license. Why *wouldn't* she go for a drive? Drive meant steel. Steel was safe.

Again, it was relative to the fey.

Shoes in hand so the heels made no sound, Katherine strolled through the kitchen, out the door, and onto the tiny sidewalk. She did not look at the prickly faery that seemed more like the landscape than a living person. She did not let her gaze linger on the whisker-thin spikes on his skin or the oddly graceful way his bulbous body moved. There was a sort of beauty in his ugliness that made her wonder if she would ever see a faery she found horrifying. Admittedly she had no pressing urge to embrace the spiny little man creature, but she had questions.

Oh, she had so very many questions! She sighed, and then quickly looked up at the sky.

For all her growing list of complaints about the desert, she could admit that the sunsets were the sort of majestic thing that made her want to paint. If she spilled a handful of bottles of paint in the air, it still wouldn't match the tangle of color that seemed to slide across the sky in some new and wondrous way night after night. The sheer size of the sky in the desert made the landscape look like it stretched on and on, and the moon hovered so near to the ground that she could believe that the land was dry only because the moon had drawn all the water into itself.

"Pretty, isn't it?"

Katherine ignored the voice.

As far as tricks went, that one was pretty basic. The fey spoke to see who could hear them. Katherine mastered ignoring faeries when she was barely out of diapers.

"Hello? ¡Hola!"

It was the brief word in Spanish that caught Katherine's attention. The fey, even the most Americanized of them, tended to speak Gaelic if they weren't speaking English. They came from a Celtic culture, and their language reflected it--but maybe that was different in the Southwest.

She glanced around, trying to find a not-entirely-awkward space between the pretense of not hearing if the speaker was fey and not looking like she was thoroughly rude if the speaker was human. Being half-fey didn't come with a "how-to" book, so in such cases, Katherine just fumbled around as best she could.

"New neighbor," the girl said, louder now. "Take out your earbuds."

Katherine fumbled at her ears as if there were earbuds in them. Her hair covered her ears, so it was a semi-believable gesture.

"Hi . . ."

"Gina." The girl stuck out her hand as if to shake. She was brash and friendly, and Katherine fumbled with it.

"Kat." She accepted the hand and tried to shake. That was another on the "don't do" list, as if she somehow wouldn't notice the person in front of her was fey. As if she'd expose her heritage by accidentally touching them.

"I was starting to think you'd never come outside. Too hot?" Gina nodded, but then continued as if Katherine had answered. "A lot of people from back East are like that. Just wait until you acclimate! Then all the 'it's a dry heat' jokes will begin."

Katherine opened her mouth.

"So what do you do in there?" Gina continued before Katherine could speak. "Like I hear the fights. Your Mom, right? Fight lady? But *that* . . ." She nodded toward the house where the gong and drum cacophony were still on high. "Make me lose my ever-loving mind, right?"

"Family." Katherine shrugged.

Maybe having a friend would be easy if she wasn't really required to talk—and Gina was a fountain of words.

"Are you too East Coast to walk?" Gina motioned. "I'm

meeting some friends. Desert's cold, got to walk when you can, right? You'll learn."

"Walk? Like . . . out there?" Katherine gestured to the scrub, Palo Verde trees, and darkened evening.

Out there was dangerous.

Out there was the domain of the faeries.

Out there was forbidden.

But, then again, so was stealing the car. Katherine vacillated. There wasn't a great answer here. She had no friends, but what if there were faeries? Should she go to protect Gina?

"Afraid of cactus? Or the coyotes? Or 'dangerous immigrants' like the news talks about?" Gina's voice took on an edge. "I was trying to be friendly, but if you have some sort of racist—"

"Whoa! No. My dad was dark," Katherine said hurriedly.

By "dark," Katherine meant he leaned toward the Dark Court, all *gancanaghs* did, but the truth was that his skin was also brown enough to have people ask intemperate questions. She was thought to be American Indian in South Dakota, Black or maybe "Mexican" (as if all of Latin America and South America was Mexico) in North Carolina. Katherine couldn't ever talk about herself in terms of what her race was, though. She wasn't any of those. She was half-fey—and that wasn't a category that humans understand. Her mom was white, but Katherine's own skin was darker because of her fey side.

The bottom line was that Katherine Miller fit exactly nowhere. She wasn't all human, all fey, actually Brown, or able to discuss any of it without lying—and oh, yeah, lies physically hurt.

She cleared her throat and said, "I was going to, umm, borrow the car and go for a drive, but I could walk."

Gina smiled. "Excellent. No one moves here, so we've been waiting to meet you."

"We?" Katherine echoed quietly.

"Those of us already trapped here," Gina said in a teasing tone. "Seriously. Unless you're a survivalist or your car breaks down or you have dreams of being a meth cooker, why in the name of all that's good would you move here?"

This was one of those moments where lying would be an excellent skill to have, but more and more, it hurt to lie. She could still do it, but it felt like Katherine would choke or cough uncontrollably, like her throat was closing when she lied. So she aimed for evasive but true.

"My mom picks where we move. Since my dad died—"

"Ouch," Gina interjected. "Sorry."

"Thanks . . . but Dad died, and so we move. Mom telecommutes or travels for work stuff and Aunt Ida is an old hippie, so . . ." Katherine shrugged. "Here we are."

As Katherine had spoken, Gina started walking. Katherine had fallen in step, trying not to look at the random faeries in the desert. They watched, but not attentively. It was more of a casual notice.

And so, Katherine thought that everything was going to be fine. She'd made a friend. She was outside. It was all a refreshing change—right up to the moment when Gina stopped at a campsite.

For whatever reason, no faeries were within the light of the fire that was burning in a metal ring, chasing away the edge of the desert cold.

Around the fire were assorted people. Three girls. Five

boys. All were around eighteen to twenty-five if she had to guess.

Then Katherine turned.

The problem was right there. A man, half-hidden by shadows. Dark hair. Dark skin. Shadows made flesh. Katherine had a fleeting thought that he was only visible because of the shadows. Had the fire extinguished, he would become one with the night. The shadow-made man clearly wasn't human, but unlike every other faery she'd met, he wasn't hidden from sight. He was flaunting his otherness like there was no threat in it.

He looked like every terrifying thing Katherine had ever wanted.

Run!

Katherine stared at him, as he watched her with the sort of focus that she'd seen from the random rattlesnakes that seemed omnipresent in the Southwest.

"Blink," Gina whispered. Then she proceeded to introduce everyone there.

As she did so, Katherine nodded, replied, and generally tried to sound like less of weirdo than she was. And all the while, she tried not to ask why *he* was watching her— because the truth was that she already knew why he watched her.

The stranger watched because Katherine wasn't human.

Just like him.

But she couldn't speak *those* words.

Finally, after what seemed like forever, Gina said, "And this is Urian."

He stood then, unfolding himself from the lawn chair as if it were a velvet sofa. He wore gloves, which she only just noticed. Any hint of doubt as to what he was would have vanished even if her ability to recognize the fey was suddenly absent. Katherine had watched her own father move that way, had seen fey her whole life. No mere human could move so gracefully. Urian, as with most fey, seemed to ripple to his feet, as if every muscle movement was a conscious choice and the air was as fluid as water.

Why gloves?

He took a step forward, eyes locked on her, and Katherine needed to run.

They chase, she reminded herself.

He took another step, and the fire highlighted features too perfect for mortals.

What do they see when they look at him? she wondered.

To her, Urian was possibly the most striking faery she'd seen. He was taller than her, a mix of taut muscles and straight spine; he held himself with the grace of a street brawler. There was a rawness to him that Katherine would typically find alluring. Add to that, cheekbones that could cut and lips curled in a smile that looked like laughter. Katherine was holding back a sigh.

The fey typically used glamours to hide or alter their appearances, though, so she wasn't sure what he looked like to regular people.

"It is an honor, Katherine." He pulled off a black leather glove before he reached for her hand.

Katherine jerked her arm back, out of his reach. She didn't touch people often or easily, *couldn't* because of what she was, and she had no idea what that would do to a faery.

Could they become addicted, too? Was it slower? Faster?

"Don't," she whispered, even though the thought of touching him, touching another faery, made her tremble.

And he smiled, a twist of lips that was more feral than not.

Katherine stepped away, out of reach, closer to safety.

He bowed his head slightly, not breaking eye contact, as if he had actually lifted her hand in his. "I am Urian."

Chapter Seven

URIAN

If guilt were a part of his make-up, Urian would feel guilty for watching the girl squirm. She was so obviously not merely mortal that he couldn't help wanting to ask her why she pretended to be one of them. He'd never pretended—not even as a child. His mother, more mortal than not, had not asked it of him.

He remembered her lessons with a burst of pride. "You must never pretend to be less than you are, Uri."

Of course, his mother had also waited in vain for his father to remember them, to stop hiding, to return to her. She'd died of a broken heart. That might not have been the term the physicians used, but it was the cause all the same.

Urian wasn't prone to such *mortal* emotions, though. Not guilt. Not longing. And certainly not love of anyone other than his mother and sister. He was the only faery outside the courts *and* Faerie itself who had the strength of a royal—and this half-mortal creature standing before him was nothing more than a pawn waiting to be used.

"Grab her a drink." Urian ordered. "And a chair."

He didn't look away from her to see if they obeyed. They would. He might not use his innate addictive nature on the lot of them, but all faeries were alluring to humans. These people were mortals, fun when the need struck him and disposable when that was for the best.

Uri, admittedly, chose to associate with humans who were interesting in some way—artists or those beautiful of voice or form. It was a flaw in his kind, unfortunately. Faeries were drawn to the unusual or striking much the way some birds were lured by shiny trinkets.

And as a *gancanagh,* Urian was innately drawn toward attractive mortals who shined like gems. Unlike his monster of a father, though, Urian didn't set out to enslave and destroy them. He'd never be the one who destroyed someone he claimed to love—even if that lack of destruction was simply because he'd chosen not to love.

He wasn't quite sure what to do with a halfling, though. Urian might not be keen on laws, but there were those lines he was aware he ought not cross. The High Queen's rules topped that list, and she had opinions on halflings. Strong ones.

"Are you shaking?" he asked the halfling, who was now looking toward the mortals in a way he could only describe as protective.

"I don't need a chair *or* a drink." Katherine folded her arms. Louder she said, "No, thank you. I'm leaving."

"I mean them no harm," he murmured. "Gina and the others. They are my friends."

"Right." Katherine gave him a disdainful look. "I always order my friends around."

"Do you have friends?" he asked before he could quell the impulse. "Lovers?"

As he waited, Urian suddenly found every plot and plan in his life uninteresting. She, however, was enchanting.

"A, None of your business. And B, even if I do, I'm not auditioning for new ones." She held his gaze in a way that was rare for him. Most people—fey and human—found him intimidating. She seemed to be undaunted.

Unexpectedly, Urian laughed at the temper in her before saying, "Pity. I give a great audition."

"At what cost to *them*?" She gestured at the others, who were openly staring. "Do they die for want of you?"

Urian startled. She obviously knew enough to recognize him for what he was. Most humans or half-humans lumped the humanoid fey in one category. How had this one so easily recognized him as *gancanagh*? Or was she suggesting that all fey left humans faery-struck?

"Perhaps you want to rescue them? Offer yourself in trade? Or advise me on a bedding schedule?" he suggested. "Tell me, pretty, what you suggest . . ."

Katherine, human though she might claim to be, glowed slightly the more she argued with him. Some hidden part of her was waking, and he wasn't about to tell her anything that made that glow vanish.

Instead, he asked, "Which ones look weakest? I wouldn't want any of them to wither for want of my attention."

"Monster." Her eyes flashed like lightning-lit obsidian.

Dark Court through and through, Urian thought with a relief he hadn't expected. He wanted her in a way that was sudden and all-consuming.

"For craving touch?" he asked. "Are you going to try to *lie* and tell me that you are above such things?"

"I don't use my friends like *that*," she retorted.

The truth was that these few mortals weren't his

bedmates at all. He was careful with them, and he'd learned when to depart. He knew the signs well enough. His own mother had been faery-struck. Thelma Foy might have denied it, but Urian had caught her staring into the shadows often enough. He knew *who* she sought. He knew who was responsible for her sorrow. Then he'd seen his niece, Moira, flee to her own death when she was faery-led.

No, Urian would not torment or kill these or *any* mortals. His rage was saved for the real monsters. His own kind. His father. The ugly truth was that after a *gancanagh* bedded a mortal, the mortal weakened when he left. His skin was the drug they couldn't find again. His touch was the poison they craved until they looked like the mortals who withered from the drugs that were prevalent in the mortal world.

Urian worked rather hard not to be a killer of mortals—although he saw no need to tell Katherine that just now. Her temper was scintillating.

He leaned closer and whispered, "Was that why you wouldn't let me touch you? Are you afraid I'll be irresistible?"

"No." She gave him a cold smile.

Urian tensed. Either she could lie with no ease, or he hadn't correctly guessed why she flinched away from him. "Come closer then."

"Over your dead body."

He laughed. Typically, he exerted the influence his kind always did on mortals—and halflings. Urian had learned that even the fey felt his allure, so they scurried to obey. Not her, though. Not the halfling who currently stared at him as if she wasn't sure whether flight or fight was wiser. His already consuming interest flared hotter.

"Will you run?" he asked.

A part of him that felt more feral even than the worse of the fey hoped she would.

"From some creep who has his *friends* enthralled? No." Katherine scoffed, adding enough fervor to her lies that a lesser man might be convinced.

"Are you certain? You look like a runner to me . . ." Urian watched her fight the urge to run, her body tense and poised for flight. The urge to fight him was a curious thing for a young woman who was clearly not as human as she pretended.

A flash of lightning inside her irises made her eyes nearly white for a moment. "I fight when I must. I don't run."

Urian pressed, "You look as if you've seen a ghost, Katherine. Do I remind you of someone? Or some*thing*?"

She didn't reply to him at all this time, and he had to wonder if there was a limit to how often she could lie successfully. Was it causing her pain? He wasn't as awful as his father, of course, but a part of him understood that he wasn't playing fair.

Another part of him didn't care. He wanted the lightning, the thrum of her hunger in her pulse, the way she parted her lips ever-so-slightly when he scored a reaction.

"Do you find me frightening for some *other* reason?" he asked, staring at her with increasing interest as each moment passed.

"No." Katherine swallowed hard at this lie. *That* was interesting. She was mortal enough to speak an actual lie.

"You do that convincingly," he admitted with respect. It was not a trait he shared.

"What?" She stared at him, chin tilting almost subconsciously. Whatever faery had sired her was one with shadows.

"Lie. Does it hurt?"

"Why would it?" Katherine was ready to fight. Her posture shifted slightly. She slid her left foot to the side, widening her stance as if steadying herself for an impending fight.

He saw no weapon, and a feral side of him—one that was very much Dark Court—liked the idea that she was willing to fight hand-to-hand.

"I suppose most of our kind don't admit to you that we see you for what you are," he said, voice pitched lower so as to keep their conversation secret. "Maybe you think we don't notice you . . ."

"I don't know what you mean." Katherine swallowed hard again, but she still successfully murmured another of her lies.

"Liar." Uri stepped up closer to her, hoping that she might strike him if provoked enough. "And you're wondering what to do . . . do you expose our little secret to these mortals? Do you wonder if they'll defend me?"

Almost against her will, she asked, "Would they?"

"What if I send them away? Give you the answers you so desperately need? Would that change the temper in those pretty brown eyes?" Urian reached out to brush her hair away, to touch her.

Katherine stopped him, knocking his hand away with a strike of her forearm. "Don't touch me. No one touches me. It's . . . not safe."

At that, Urian suddenly had more questions than he could fathom. *Not safe?* What exactly caused a pretty half-faery woman to be dangerous to touch? Had she been told lies? Or was she correct? Whatever the reason, it did nothing to erase his interest in her.

"Just . . . leave me alone," Katherine muttered, turning and taking a step away from him. "Seriously. I won't bother you. You don't bother me. Okay? Pax. Peace. Truce. Whatever."

Gina returned then. She held out a bottle of water and can of some sort of carbonated fruit juice. "Everything okay?"

"Mmm." Katherine affixed a not-at-all-convincing smile. "I thought I . . . recognized your friend. Sorry."

"Uri?" Gina grinned. "He's not exactly forgettable, is he? We met when—"

"Gina." Urian interrupted. "Katherine obviously knows a few of my relatives, so she was caught off-guard by my presence. She *saw* me for what I am."

Gina's eyes widened. "For real?"

Urian nodded. "She knows what I am."

"You can see faeries?" Gina practically breathed the words.

"No," Katherine started. "Not really. Faeries are a myth, and I think it's probably best if I just leave and—"

"Can you really *see* them?" Gina blurted. "The faeries? I mean, I believe Uri and all, but as much as I look for them, I never see anyone. I try, but it's knowing they're out there isn't the same as having the Sight and . . . we can't make the ointment."

"You *want* to see faeries?" Katherine's voice was thin and breathy now, barely a whisper in the dark desert, as if she'd been exercising at length, and Urian had a flicker of longing to hear her sound that way for reasons other than fear.

"Can I tell her the rest?" Gina asked Urian. "Please?"

Urian shrugged, watching Katherine's expression with interest. She was completely unprepared for their secret to be exposed. Most fey were. They had been taught to hide, as if there was some shame in being greater-than-mortal.

"Urian is an exiled faery prince," Gina announced in a squeaky voice.

"He's *what*?" Katherine took another step backward.

"A faery prince." Gina stared at Urian with the sort of awe that made him reconsider whether or not he needed to move on.

"Ha. Faeries aren't . . . real." Katherine's tone was drawn in pain now. Her hands were clenched in fists, and a thin sheen of sweat had her looking like she was glowing in the firelight. She might be able to lie, but, apparently, it wasn't *easy* for her to do so this often.

Reluctant respect filled Urian.

"Faeries can't lie, Katherine. Surely, you've heard *that*, at the least," he teased. "I am exactly that. A faery prince. Exiled. A man without a throne. . ."

Gina sighed.

"Uh huh. And I'm a talking chihuahua trapped in a human suit," Katherine drawled.

Urian smiled at her. "Join us. We'll talk awhile, and you can learn all about the fey."

She shook her head.

"I know it seems impossible," Gina started. "Here in the middle of nowhere. A real live faery prince!"

"You're drunk," Katherine whispered. This time she didn't wince because she was looking at Gina and the others, who *were* rather intoxicated.

Drunk or not, they were also truthful—and she knew it.

"Gina." Urian opened his arms, inviting the mortal girl to his side. She came easily and happily. They always did. "Let

Katherine go for now. Perhaps she just needs time to think. Not everyone is as eager to believe as you were."

Both Gina and Katherine looked crestfallen at his reply, and Urian felt a foolish flicker of hope that Katherine's expression held jealousy at seeing Gina in his embrace. She likely didn't, but she'd be much easier to manage if she did.

Silently she turned and walked away, not once looking back. He wondered if she still wanted to run, and that was why it was so difficult to let her leave--or if the urge to chase her was simply because she might be the ally he'd sought. Either way he was far from done with Katherine.

And he was fairly certain that she realized it, too.

Chapter Eight

AISLINN

Now that Aislinn had left Seth resting in her chambers, she slid from who she was able to be with him and who she had to become with her court. Sometimes that transition felt like donning a mask. Sometimes it felt more natural than being around mortals. There was a part of her that still thought and felt mortal, but she was the living embodiment of Summer itself. That came with a level of languor and a level of temper that were constant reminders that she was not the mortal she had thought she'd been when she met Seth.

Today, she was more relaxed than she otherwise would be simply due to the fact that her beloved was home and had spent the night demonstrating how much he missed her.

"My queen?" Tavish, her now-healed advisor, prompted as she strolled into the room. With him were Siobhan, as well as the former Dark King and the current Dark King.

"Seth came home unexpectedly," Aislinn offered with a shrug. "All is well. I was simply otherwise occupied." She gave them all a wry look as she added, "His *mother* sent him to me."

Despite the edge in her voice, Tavish didn't reply. Later, when she was feeling maudlin about Seth's constant absence, they'd discuss it. For now, the Summer Queen motioned for her advisors to depart. Tavish was healed, but he wasn't needed for this. Not that she didn't trust him, but this conversation was not for anyone to know yet.

She settled on the floor of the greenhouse-like room, so the two tiny tiger cubs—which Irial had sent to her as gifts—could reach her. The cubs rolled and romped as if they'd always been a part of the Summer Court.

"Sorcha knew he was coming here," Irial muttered.

"Exactly," Aislinn said.

"She *sent* him, Iri," Niall, the current Dark King, corrected. "Of course Sorcha knew Seth was here."

"No, love, Sorcha knew my *son* was coming *here*." Irial scowled. "She sent Seth here because she knew of Urian's intentions. She had to have seen what was liable to happen with Urian. So she sent Seth to calm Aislinn's rage. It was a wise move. Summer can be temperamental."

"Sitting right here," Aislinn reminded the older faeries. Then she looked at the Dark King and asked, "How much of an incident will it be if I am attacked again? And if I defend myself against . . . him?"

"Less so than if Winter intervenes," Irial muttered. "You are, at the least, family to Urian. As his great-niece, you could posit that this was merely family squabbles. His actions would not be the same if Urian were to strike Winter. If he attacks *them*, there will be consequences."

"As would there be if he were to attack my court," Niall added mildly, and Aislinn took a strange comfort at seeing the abyss guardians—seemingly sentient shadows--cling to him and his consort as he continued, "Winter or Dark would not be so tolerant with Urian as you are being."

"But you're . . ." Aislinn gestured between the two men, not quite knowing the words here. They weren't wed, but there was no one who could doubt their bond.

"In love? Setting up a future? Enjoying naked hours together?" the current Dark King suggested. "Nothing there is official, Aislinn. Whatever I feel or do not feel for Irial—"

"He loves me," Irial interjected with a smug look. "Despite my many *many* flaws, he loves me. He even admits it sometimes."

Aislinn bit back a laugh at Niall's frustrated expression. The Dark King—once advisor to her court—was not forthright or public with affections, but he'd become unhinged when Irial was attacked and hovering on the edge of permanent death. There was no doubt of their feelings.

The Dark King still glanced at Irial and said, "*Must* you interrupt me?"

"You're basically her grandfather now, too, you know. It's important for children to see examples of loving relationships." Irial folded his arms and gave Niall a chastising look. "You know that. I bookmarked several chapters."

"He's reading parenting books," Niall muttered to Aislinn. "He's started a list of what he calls 'love affirmations'—gifts, acts of service, quality time."

The Summer Queen laughed. For most of her life she'd been afraid of the Dark Court, but there was something in the way they loved that was more familiar to her than the High Court or Winter Court ever could be. Dark Court love was all-consuming, destroy-the-world, grand gesture.

"I'll have you both know I'm being perfectly reasonable,"

Irial said, beaming at her. "I have missed so much time with you, though. I will be an excellent grandfather to you. You just wait."

"I didn't agree . . ." Aislinn flinched a little at not knowing what fathers or grandfathers exactly *did*. She'd never had a father or a grandfather, and the idea of accepting what was tantamount to an alliance with the Dark Court made her pause.

"Could we please address the topic at hand?" Niall's tone was stern, but no one there could miss the look in his eyes as he glanced at the embodiment of Chaos. The Dark King was in agreement that Irial would be a fabulous grandfather— and very visibly in love with him.

"Urian thinks he has a legitimate claim to my throne and yours," Aislinn said, grateful for the save. She scooped one of the tiger cubs into her arms. "Does he?"

"Not in my opinion." Niall's abyss guardians snapped out, protecting his boots from the other tiger cub, which kept trying to bite and claw the leather. "I was declared the next Dark King centuries before this boy was born."

"You rejected it. You left me," Irial reminded him. "My fault, but you offered fealty to the Summer, so . . . when he was born--"

"And yet, here I am, Irial. The Dark Court is mine. Any attacks against my sovereignty will be met with extreme clarification." Niall's tone made Aislinn grateful that they had a peace of sorts between their courts.

"And *my* throne? Does his claim against the Summer Court have any merit?"

Aislinn was fairly sure that Urian had to have some measure of legitimacy to his claim, but she needed the confirmation of those who were far more adept at the last thousand years of faery history. These two were—because they'd lived through it.

"The curse I made –stealing half of the young Summer King's power and placing it in a mortal family line, *your* line, Ash--wasn't explicitly that the kingling needed to look for a faery *queen*. The curse was that the power was hidden in your family. If Keenan had been open to a male partner, he'd have been romancing both men and women for centuries, but well . . ." Irial snorted. "Keenan is strictly heterosexual, so it was technically only hidden in the women of the Foy family."

"Could Urian have taken the throne ever? He's a Foy. So when Thelma died . . .?" Aislinn asked.

"If Keenan chose Urian? Yes." Irial looked smug. "I knew that he wouldn't, and so the Summerlight passed to the occasional son. Keenan, of course, was not thinking clearly. Not all *queens* are women."

Niall sighed. "He's also been learning 'modern terms' since you're still a veritable toddler."

Aislinn's smile was tense. "I'm not a toddler."

"Not even half a century," Niall retorted.

"And yet," she echoed his words. "Here I am, Niall. The Summer Court is mine."

Irial chortled, scooped up the other tiger cub, and gave it a wallet to chew on.

"Is that *hetero* part a, umm, a Summer Court thing?" Aislinn felt her cheeks burn with lingering mortal awkwardness, but it wasn't like there was a handbook on life as a faery and most of her court seemed to be less flexible in partners than the High Court and Dark Court.

And sometimes I feel like a child for asking any of it, Aislinn thought. *A toddler, indeed.*

"Summer Court and Winter Court are often more

limited in their intimacies," Niall said levelly, as if there was nothing strange in her asking him. "Not strictly so, but the court reflects the regent. The last regent of your court, Keenan, favored his accursed mother in seeking both a heterosexual and monogamous future. And the regent before Keenan was equally narrow in his thinking. Solitary, Dark, and High . . . not so much. The Winter Court is the only court that veers towards monogamy, which could have been what influenced Keenan in those limitations. Or the curse? It's hard to say."

Seth, Aislinn thought far too quickly. *Was he interested in other people? Mortals? Men? He'd spent so much time with Niall. And in the High Court.*

Seth was the nominal leader of the Solitary Faeries, but he was also aligned to both the High Court and the Dark Court.

. . . which meant he was rarely here for her. Seth might not see an issue with that, but more and more, Aislinn did.

Problems for another day, she reminded herself.

Aislinn darted a glance at Niall. She'd never asked questions about anything strictly private, but *gancanaghs* like Niall —and Irial, as well—were addictive. Seth had been mortal when the former Summer King had pushed Niall to spend an excess of time with him.

"Keenan wanted you to seduce Seth away from me," Aislinn murmured.

Niall had the sort of expression that meant that his patience was wearing thin. "We are where we are *now*, Ash. I'm trying to be your friend here—and not only because of Leslie or because of Irial. As your friend I will ask that we focus on the topic, not lingering insults against either of our courts. We are at peace with the Winter Court. That will change if Urian strikes one of us."

"Right. What do we do about Urian?" Aislinn asked, mentally shoving her questions away. "I'm not seeking violence against anyone, but I will not allow him to injure my faeries. He needs to understand that there are limits to what we can tolerate. Striking me or mine invites retribution."

"Let me go talk to my son," Irial suggested. "Maybe—"

"No," Niall and Aislinn said in unison.

"Not your place," Niall added, almost apologetically. "If Urian comes to my court, he will not walk away uninjured. If he strikes mine—and that includes my . . ." He gestured at Irial. "I will send The Hunt to retrieve him for me, so we might discuss matters."

"But . . ." Aislinn looked at Irial.

Irial looked heartbroken, but he said nothing. The former Dark King, however, was subject of no court. He was a free agent. Would he risk the love he had with Niall to save his son?

"Court first," Niall said coldly. "I defend what's *mine* at all costs. I suggest you do the same for the Summer Court. If you would like—as a gesture of goodwill—I would lend the Hunt to you to find he who has struck down your guard."

Aislinn paused, looking between them. "Let me ponder. I feel like waiting rather than acting is not the right course."

Niall gave a short nod. "Summer is impulsive that way."

It was not a judgment, merely an acknowledgment of truth. Each faery belonged somewhere. Some were solitary, preferred to forego a court's protection. Some were born to a court and stayed. Others chose. No matter how they elected their affinity, ever faery was what they aligned with in the world: Dark Court's wicked shadows, Summer Court's frolicking sunlight, or Winter Court's calmer snowfalls. Each could rage, but their instinctual reactions tended toward their alignments.

Why resist?

"Send me the Hunt, if you will," Aislinn accepted the offer. "He struck mine. I owe them safety."

Almost guiltily she reached out for Irial's hand. "Forgive me?"

"My son drew first blood, but I'll ask for mercy," Irial said. "If he had hurt you, or Niall, or Leslie, I don't know that I'd be so calm."

Shadows radiated out from Niall. "Or you. His rage is at *you*, Irial, and at the Summer Queen. I will not allow anyone to strike me."

"Other than you," Irial said lightly, tone teasing and flirtatious. "Or Leslie. She can strike me if she chooses."

Niall waved the words away. "You know what I mean, Irial. Now is not the time to—"

"To hurt Irial needs only hurting you or Leslie," Aislinn interrupted, trying to think strategically. "To hurt me is to hurt Seth."

"And anger *Sorcha*?" Irial laughed. "No. The whelp is fine. No worries there."

"Keep yourself safe, Irial. And Leslie," Aislinn said mildly. "And, Niall, if you are willing, send me the Hunt. I have quarry."

Chapter Nine

KATHERINE

Katherine slipped out of the house several days later. Gina, her neighbor, was waiting there. She looked friendly enough, but any mortal foolish enough to consort with a faery made of darkness was of questionable intellect.

"I don't want to discuss him," Katherine said as the girl stood and approached.

"Fair." Gina fell in step beside Katherine.

As they walked, Katherine started to relax. She really *did* want friends. There was introvert, and then there was weird-secluded-loner, and Katherine wasn't *naturally* either one. If she had a choice, she suspected she'd be as extrovert as a person could get. Wander. Meet people. Seduc—*no*, not that. She wasn't like her dad. She chose to be mortal.

After several tense, silent moments, Gina asked, "Could we discuss how you were glowing?"

"Glowing?"

"Like you were coated in something, and Uri was a black light making you shine." Gina shrugged, but her expression was intense. "Are you actually human?"

Katherine sighed, looking out at the faeries lounging in among the rocks and Palo Verde trees and squat muted green shrubs that she'd learned were called sagebrush. The fey things were pointedly not looking at her, and she had to wonder if that was Uri's doing.

"Not totally," Katherine admitted.

Panic hit her hard as soon as she said the words. Never admit. Never risk. Never leave the house. She'd lived over two decades by those rules—all because her father was a *gancangh*, a love-faery, a seducer. But it had hit her like a slap that she was never going to get more mortal. *Her* Sight wasn't because of some ointment. It was because she wasn't human. Not really.

"My dad was. . . you know." Katherine swallowed hard. Maybe it was easier admitting it because Gina already believed in the fey.

"So you're basically destined to be stuck between worlds, eh?" Gina nudged her with her shoulder. "Maybe the desert *is* where you ought to be. We get the lost ones here, in-betweeners of some sort or another."

Katherine nodded.

"So you know a lot of people like you?" Gina prompted.

"None."

"Until Uri," Gina added.

Again, Katherine nodded. "Don't really *know* him though, do I?"

Gina gave her a wicked grin. "Girl, from the way he was eye-stripping you, you certainly *could*. Don't think we haven't all wished he'd look at us that way, but he says we'd get sick —like AIDS but worse—if we touch him."

Katherine nodded. "Truth."

"Of course, it is. Faeries can't lie." Gina rolled her eyes.

"But if his touch is addictive and yours is, too, what does that mean? Are faery couples like . . . storms?"

Briefly Katherine thought about her parents. They weren't both fey, but they'd definitely been intense together. Sharing a house with them meant needing a yard or headphones. They were ridiculous.

A flicker of a thought of what that would mean for two *gancanaghs* made her need to clear her throat and look away. Her brain quickly filled in "Urian" in the visual that flashed to mind.

Just because he's the only other gancanagh I've met, she consoled herself, but even the thought was enough of a lie for her to flinch.

"I wouldn't know what two faeries are like together," Katherine finally said. "But, you know, not all faeries are addictive the way . . . he would be if . . ."

"If you did whatever you were just thinking?" Gina teased.

Despite everything, or maybe because of it, Katherine laughed. "Shut up."

"Uh huh. We all think it. He's a fucking prince. Smart. Sweet. Sexy." Gina fanned herself with her hand. "I wasn't even sure I could like guys until him. Mostly, I'm all about women, but Uri . . ." She shrugged. "I guess if I was going to have a straight-curious moment it might as well be a faery prince."

Katherine paused at the defensiveness in Gina's tone. There was an edge, a fuck-you-if-you-reject-me thread there that Katherine thought she could stand to adopt. "I wish I could say that about what *I am* with your attitude."

Gina gave her a weird look.

"Faery. I never admitted it before today, but in fairness, I don't get out much so maybe I would've if I had more opportunities. My mother is protective."

"Because she's human?" Gina asked.

"Yeah. And my father was . . . I mean, they were so in love it was like an ice cream headache sometimes. All the sweet. All the cold. They fought sometimes, but even then . . . just in love like it was their jobs." Katherine shook her head. "Then he died. And she's left with me. Not quite human. Not quite *not*. We thought I could be hidden, especially because we thought they didn't notice me, but I guess that's not really true, is it?"

"Urian knew exactly what you are," Gina added.

"He knew I was fey which isn't the same as knowing exactly what I am." Katherine motioned toward the town. "Show me around."

Gina paused, clearly with more to say, but she didn't press the matter. Instead of asking about faeries or cheering for Urian, she gave Katherine a confused look and said, "But you've lived here a while now . . ."

"Like I said, I don't get out much."

They didn't do anything terribly exciting. They looked at a used bookshop and browsed a rock shop.

Then Katherine paused, a geode in hand and Gina's chatter at her side. This was probably the most active thing Katherine had done since moving to New Mexico. At the least, it was the single most independent thing she'd done. Her family worried too much if she left the apartment alone.

What will they do when I leave for real?

If I am recognizable as fey, I can't hide. I don't know how to live as a faery, though.

"Coffee?" Gina asked, interrupting her reverie.

"What?" Katherine put the rock back on the shelf carefully.

"Caffeine. Coffee? Tea? Soda? I need something." Gina motioned toward the door. "Do you drink any of those things?"

"Whatever has sugar sounds good to me."

"Sweet tooth, huh?" Gina teased.

"I think so . . ." Katherine shook her head. Traditionally, sugar wasn't appealing, but she could recall her father at the kitchen table spooning so much sugar into his tea that her teeth ached at the sight, even as a child.

I'm changing.

Sugar sounded almost as good as touching Urian's arm.

Who gets excited about an arm, for goodness sake?

Katherine shoved those thoughts away, but she knew she was shifting inside and wasn't sure why. Was it meeting another faery? She'd grown up with one, so that seemed wrong. Was it an age thing? Mid-twenties didn't seem terribly significant.

All she knew for sure as she followed Gina into a diner was that the need to wander was pressing in ways that were both sudden and exciting. She was becoming less human, and in the process, she felt an insistent urge to be . . . somewhere, anywhere, not held by walls.

Chapter Ten

AISLINN

Inside a room that seemed more jungle than anything indoors ought to be, the Summer Queen was pacing. As she walked, blossoms burst forth, and for one moment--as sorrow filled her at the thought of those she loved being in peril--lightning and thunder rolled through the indoor garden.

Gram is safe.

Seth is safe.

What about the rest?

The odd truth was that the Winter Court regent and her consort—the faery who had once cursed Aislinn by choosing her—were friends of a sort. Leslie, consort to the Dark King, was a friend from before all of the changes in their lives. What would happen to the Dark King if she were hurt? Or to Donia if Keenan were?

Or to the Dark King *and* Aislinn if Irial were?

Aislinn felt embarrassed that the whole situation frightened her so. She was barely an adult in mortal years, but she was *not* mortal at all. She'd lost that via a curse that had stolen the mortality of countless other girls. Her attempted —and nearly successful—seducer had stolen her humanity, her future, and in return, she'd walked into battle to face one of the first faeries.

One would think that after such things, peace would come.

And in its way, it had, but faeries were capricious creatures, and Aislinn by birth and by curse was a faery. That "by birth" part felt like an accidental curse of its own. Sure, it meant her grandmother, who was well over one hundred years old despite looking not quite half that, was still alive.

It meant Aislinn was better able to learn how to manage her newfound powers and court.

It meant she had relatives.

And that was the trouble. Her grandfather, former Dark King and now the embodiment of Chaos, was enough of an upset to the delicate balance between the courts. Now to have a contender to *her throne?* What was she to do with that?

"Do you need space or distraction?" Seth asked.

Aislinn looked up to find her beloved watching her. He was not going to hate her no matter what she chose. Sometimes, she honestly thought he had adapted to the world they were in now better than she had done.

"I have had more than enough space," she said, hoping they could finally discuss this—or perhaps just wanting to discuss her life instead of her reign.

"I'm here now," Seth said lightly.

Sometimes she wished he could be more focused on them, on what she felt like figuring everything out on her own. Then she felt guilty. He'd become a faery for her.

Shouldn't that be enough? They were still together. They had eternity now. And he was content.

But I'm not, a small voice whispered. She couldn't even say what she wanted other than *more.* More time. More support. More love.

"What's your plan for dealing with the attack?" Seth asked.

"I've asked for the Hunt," Aislinn admitted.

"Rightly. You were attacked in your home." Seth stayed in the doorway. "And how does the Dark feel about this?"

"Niall offered them to me." She shrugged, biting back her sense that Seth ought not care what the Dark Court felt. He ought to ask how she felt.

Seth nodded. "Better you hunt Urian than Niall. If *you* attack Irial's son, you are protected from Irial's rage because you are his blood family. Having you strike preemptively is wise on Niall's part. Did he call you 'impulsive' to goad you? Or appeal to your youth? Suggest I am in danger . . .?"

Aislinn sighed. "Your logical side is *vexing.*"

Seth chuckled. "Tell me that next time you have an exam and want a study-buddy."

Heat flushed Aislinn's face. *Exams!* Her decision to take political science, history, and business classes was a source of awkwardness in the court, but Aislinn responded to outside schedules—and time in the mortal world. Unlike Leslie, Aislinn was slow at pursuing her studies, but she *was* ruling a court of impulse driven faeries at the same time. Leslie has pushed the faeries she loved away to take time to figure out what she wanted.

"What a mess I make of my life," Aislinn whispered. "I can't make it to my classes half the time, and I'm not sure what I'm to do about my murderous uncle. I thought the faery queen business was to be *fun?*"

"Melodramatic much?" Seth teased, dismissing her stress yet again.

"Murderous. Uncle," Aislinn repeated.

"Is the world ending?" Seth finally came into the room. "Tonight? Tomorrow?"

"No, but—"

"Have you already faced Winter? War? *Death?*" Seth sat on the earthen floor and pulled her into his lap. "Successfully?"

"Yes, but—"

"Life is change, Ash." Seth brushed her hair back, as if petting her. "Seasons. People. Lives evolve. We all will change, and with centuries before us . . . change can be exciting."

"He wants my throne. Urian. He wants to take it," Aislinn said. Birds swept into the room, as if her upset was a thing they could chase away with wings and song. "My throne. My court."

"Then you can demonstrate your power by way of the Hunt," Seth said lightly.

He kissed her neck—and she melted. For everything that was wrong between them, this part they had figured it pretty well. And as much as it pained her to admit, maybe part of the problem was that she wanted more of this.

"Scary, sexy, faery lady . . ." Seth murmured between kisses.

"I am," Aislinn reminded him, thinking of the way she felt when Bananach—the embodiment of War—was at her mercy. "I will kill for this court."

"I know. It's why you won't lose the throne," Seth said,

words whispering across her throat. "But let's talk about the things we can do while we wait on the Hunt."

Aislinn laughed. Her panic, her sorrows, everything that felt like it would crush her was easier to cope with when Seth was lowering her to soil and flowers. Something about sex made her feel more powerful, more invincible. If she had her way, not a single day would pass without sex.

He made quick work of her jeans and blouse.

"Naked in the greenhouse, Ash?" he teased as he stripped. "Again?"

"I don't know how it keeps happening. I start out wearing clothes, and it's like they vanish when you get near me . . ."

"Thank goodness." He tugged her panties off before setting about to removing any stress she'd once had.

When he paused, looking up at her from between her thighs, he said, "Eternity, Ash. That's what we have now."

The thought of forever like this seemed like exactly what she wanted. Happy, in love, and writhing in a greenhouse filled with proof that the Summer Court was strong again.

Aislinn pulled Seth upward, so he was on top of her and inside her. Sometimes it was very, *very* good to be queen.

Chapter Eleven

KATHERINE

Katherine spent the next week or two thinking back to the meeting with Urian—and wondering why meeting him had made the changes in her escalate. She felt like there was a whispering demand rising in her. She had to roam, go, meet people. She'd heard her own father's angry words trying to explain that very need to her mother. It was part of what he was, part of what she was becoming, and it had come over her suddenly.

Since meeting Urian.

Katherine knew why it had sparked in her. Her faery aspects were becoming increasingly obvious, and she was hiding in her room as much as she could. Studying. Reading. Staring at the faery who had taken up position outside her current home like a beautiful, wild guard dog.

And ignoring him.

That world, the world of the fey was hers too, but she couldn't break her mother's heart—or risk being captured by the faeries who tormented halflings.

So she studied and read.

She had plenty of time to do so. Her college classes were online, and her social life had the pulse of a century-dead goat. Aside from fighting with her mother or reading every folklore book she could find, Katherine had nothing really to fill her hours. Her outing with Gina was fun, but not a thing she could do often.

The next morning, Katherine felt like she had made a choice, so all that was left was acting on it.

"Video games in fifteen," Aunt Ida sung out as she passed Katherine's room.

Was this it? Her life? Trapped in the prison of her home for the rest of her . . . who knew how many decades? What about hikes? Hot air balloon rides? Horseback? Activities that weren't simply for preparedness of potential future attacks? What about having a life?

Or falling in love?

Katherine was as patient as she could be, but it seemed unfair that her mother's choice to risk it all on love meant that Katherine was to be an eternal prisoner.

She went to the window and stared out at the scrub that stretched out in the desert. There, watching her again, was Urian.

He sat on a throne of sorts, if the cheap refuse of humanity could be called a throne. Today, it was an old recliner instead of a battered lawn chair. This time, the chair was deep red leather, with a slice on the side that had left the leather parted like a battle wound.

He ought to look silly sitting there, languidly sprawled out in an old chair. Hell, he ought to look as desperate as the old, drunk creepers in trailer parks she'd stayed in a few times.

He didn't.

"What are you staring at?" her mother asked from the doorway to the room.

"Nothing . . . important."

"You tighten your throat muscles when you lie," her mom said, coming into the room. "You didn't use to do that."

Katherine looked out at Urian, who patted the arm of the chair as if beckoning a dog.

Reflexively, she flipped him off.

"So, you make vulgar gestures at nothing? Or are we admitting you lied?" Her mother's arm went around her waist.

Katherine sighed.

"Talk to me, Kitty Kat." Her mom squeezed her in a one-armed hug, still giving her space to move away.

"I went out for a walk a couple weeks ago . . ."

"I know. I saw it on the cameras." Her mother stared out the window. "There's someone out there. Do we need to pack?"

"No." Katherine pulled away from her mother and walked away from the window. "*You* don't. I need to go, though. I need to find out what--"

"*Who*. Not what." Octavia was no longer calm. "You are not a *what*."

"I'm not just a who," Katherine said, voice as non-confrontational as she could make it. "Let me go, Mom. I'm not a kid. I'm twenty-four and—"

"For a . . . for your *father* . . . twenty was still a kid. Some creatures don't mature as fast as I do, for example. Maturity in faeries—emotional maturity is complicated. The same is true of halflings. It's about life expectancy and—"

"I know." Katherine took a steadying breath. "I'm not *just* like him though, am I?"

Her mother looked away.

"I need answers I can't get here. Answers you can't give me." Katherine wished she could lie easily, but the fact that she couldn't meant that she needed her mother to look at her now, to see that she was being honest. "Mom? Watch me. You *know* when I'm honest."

When her mother looked back at her, Katherine said, "I swear I'll be careful. I swear I'll do my best to come home to you and—"

"No promises." Her mother's hand covered her mouth. "Sometimes they're binding and . . ."

Katherine nodded before gently pulling her mother's hand away.

"I just want to keep you safe," her mother said.

"And I want to have a future outside a cage," Katherine admitted. "I remember how happy you were with Dad, but I also know that if he had left you . . . if he had seduced you and left . . ."

"He didn't seduce me." Her mother sat on the edge of Katherine's bed, delicate and fierce, as if she were a tiny bird of prey.

"Really not wanting to talk about my parents' sex life, Mom. I heard enough of it to scar me." Katherine smiled at her mother to soften the words.

Not discussing it wasn't exactly working because it was at the crux of things. Katherine's genetics meant she was walking poison to humans, and she had no grasp of her lifespan, of if she was truly in peril from the fey. Her father had sworn she was, but was that true?

Or was he an overprotective dad?

"I'm going out today." Katherine walked over to the closet and started to sort through clothes. She never tossed things because she didn't know from year to year where she'd live.

"I wish you wouldn't." Her mother watched, worrying as she had for as long as Katherine could recall, but not overtly refusing.

She'd kept Katherine home, treating her like a child well past the age that such things were normal—but Katherine had allowed it by her very complacence. In all the world, it had been just them and Aunt Ida these past few years. Before that, it was them and Katherine's father.

"I'm not leaving today, but soon . . . it's time." Katherine tried the words on her tongue.

"Your father used to talk about the compulsion." Octavia looked at her now. "That sometimes he'd just need to roam or seduce . . . the way people experience hunger or thirst. The more you ignore it, the worse it grows."

"Did he . . . when you were married . . . did he . . ." Katherine felt like her whole body was on fire with embarrassment. Asking about her parents' sex life? Still weird. Still not things she wanted to know, but at the same time? Her father was the sort of faery she was. The older she got, the more obvious it was.

"Not all the way," her mother murmured. "He flirted, prowled a bit, but he didn't *bed* them. He was worried about . . ."

"Killing them," Katherine finished. "I don't want that either."

"You met someone." Her mother twisted her hands together and shot a glare toward the window.

She couldn't see him though, the man who had convinced Katherine that there were answers to be had.

It's not about him, Katherine thought, ignoring the tightening of her throat. "I don't know that it's about *him*, but he offered me answers."

"If he—or she—is a faery, I think they'll survive your, err, affections." Her mother stood. "You know I disapprove, right?"

"I do." Katherine swallowed against her tightening throat because the truth was that if her mother had disapproved as much as she said she did, those words wouldn't feel like lies.

"You have a ten o'clock curfew." Her mother stepped in and kissed her on both cheeks. "I used to tell your father to be careful, to come home to me, to remember what would happen to me if he left too long. And I told him not to hurt anyone."

Katherine nodded.

"But Kitty Kat, I don't *care* what happens to them"—Octavia waved her hand toward the window—"when it comes to you. I'll slaughter the world to keep *you* safe. If you need to exorcise this at his expense, whoever he is, so be it."

Katherine stared silently at her mother.

"What's his name?"

"His . . ." Katherine glanced back out the window. Urian still sat there in his makeshift throne watching her window.

He lifted his hand toward her, beckoning.

Katherine slammed the steel shutters closed, muffling a cry as the toxic metal singed her hand tonight.

"Katherine!" Octavia was across the room in a blink, grabbing Katherine's now-bloody hand.

The smell of burning flesh worsened.

"You're—"

"Changing," Katherine finished. "Something happened when I meet Urian. That's his name. Maybe it was coincidence, but I feel increasingly more . . . like dad since we met."

"Urian," her mother repeated. "What do you know of him?"

Katherine laughed awkwardly before saying, "He *says* he's an exiled prince, and he has human friends—or subjects maybe? I don't even know."

"Which court?"

Of all the replies that her mother could've made, Katherine wasn't expecting that one. She sort of blinked at her. Her very mortal mother claimed not to know much of the workings of the world of the fey.

But mortals could lie, couldn't they?

Mutely, Katherine simply stared at her mother, who was scowling at the shutters.

"Summer? Winter? Dark? Shadow? High?" Her mother frowned. "I don't recall your father mentioning any exiled princes. There *was* a bound king . . . but his name was Keenan."

"So . . . you know a bit more than you've shared, then?" Katherine was shaken by the wave of betrayal. "Even now, you didn't think I was old enough to learn all this?"

"Kitty Kat . . ."

Ignoring her, Katherine grabbed a bag. Jeans and a shirt were perfectly fine. She wasn't dressing up for a date. What difference did it make what she wore? She wasn't trying to impress the faux prince. She was simply hunting for answers —some of which her mother, apparently, had hidden.

"Katherine!"

But for one of the few times in her twenty-odd years, Katherine wasn't interested in stopping. She'd known her mother was protective, known she was training Katherine for all sorts of disasters, but for reasons that really had made logical sense, Katherine assumed that part of that training was sharing everything she knew.

Apparently not.

She wasn't going to trust everything Urian said, but today Katherine was going to give in to instincts that weren't entire human. Tonight, she was going to embrace being her father's daughter.

Chapter Twelve

URIAN

Urian watched her walk toward him. He was put off that it had taken almost sixteen days for her to come out of her tower, and he desperately wanted her to feel as needy as he did—or maybe he wanted to *not* feel this needy. He wasn't sure. All he could say for certain was that he felt a compulsion, an unpleasant pull toward her.

"Stalker much?" she said, as if there was something wrong with his attention.

Instead of answering Katherine, he pulled out an old pocket watch that had long since stopped working and looked at it. Time was fleeting, even for one of the fey. He knew it with a surety that had carried him along for over a century.

She looked as exasperated as he felt. "You sit there staring at me for two weeks and—"

"You live here?" He looked around, as if surprised, and teased, "Who knew?"

She flipped her middle finger up and walked away. She

had a good walk, hips swaying in time to ancient rhythms and posture fit for a battlefield. It gave him pause.

"Whose get are you? What faery? What court? Or are you sired by a solitary faery?"

She stopped mid-step and looked over her shoulder. "*Get? Sired?* I'm not an animal, Urian. I'm a person. Like you."

His pulse quickened rebelliously at the sound of his name on her lips. Pushing that traitorous longing aside, he stood. "*How* much like me, Katherine of Miller?"

"Just Katherine." She sounded terse, but she'd stopped walking away.

Slowly, intentionally putting all the lust of a *gancanagh* into his every step, he prowled toward her. And as she watched him with a look that seemed more predator-in-waiting than he was expecting, he added, "Do you think I would lay siege to a *random* tower, Just Katherine?"

She swallowed, and he saw the same traitorous interest in her lightning-flecked eyes. "Katherine. Or Kat."

"I stayed here in heat and dark, left with nothing but myself for company," he continued. "Do you suppose I pay such favor to everyone, Katherine or Kat?"

"I know what you're doing," she said with a strange tremble.

"And what am I doing, Katherine?" He reached out, taking her hand in his.

"What . . .?" Katherine started to pull her hand away, and her entire body glowed as if the moon had somehow slipped into her body. She was a light that every fey thing for miles must notice.

Her voice was as shaky as he felt as she asked, "What's happening?"

Mine.

Urian's arm went around her as her knees buckled. He wasn't letting go.

Ever.

"I'm going to kiss you." He told himself it was merely a ploy, that he was simply using what tools he had, that he wasn't seducing her for any reason other than entrapping her to aid in his cause. But Urian couldn't lie the way she could. He wanted her the way he had never wanted anyone—or anything. This was all that mattered.

He leaned closer, lowering his mouth to steal a kiss.

One kiss.

What would it hurt? His cause was just, and if she was mortal enough to become enthralled, he'd tend to her needs as she fought at his side.

The moment his lips brushed hers, not even enough to call it a kiss, Katherine jerked away.

"Dangerous," she croaked out.

"I'm not dangerous to *you*. I don't want to hurt you," he swore, not a trace of mistruth in the words. "And you, my lovely, are not a mortal."

"No. I'm dangerous to you." She took several steps away from him, even as her hand touched her lips. "I can't."

"I'm safe. . . unless your lips are coated with poison. Are they?"

She shook her head. "I am. All of me."

Urian would laugh, but she sounded so sincere. Was this a result of misinformation about faeries?

"You aren't immune to lust. Are you, Katherine?" He watched her continue to back away, and it did nothing for the raging need he felt toward her. "Come with me. Give me this day and night, and I'll answer every question you have.

You won't regret it, Kat. I swear this to you. No maiden or experienced woman ever has. No man either."

Lightening flashed brightly enough in her eyes that he thought she might not be able to see around it. She felt the same fierce longing he did. Whatever had happened when he first took her hand, she'd felt it too.

"I won't abandon you," he promised, words he had never offered freely. He held out his hand to her, brushing her fingertips to see if that was enough to elicit another wave of desire.

It was.

"Please? Give me your day and night," he asked, nearly begging now.

"Wait! You're a *gancanagh,* too." She stared at him in a way that wasn't lust-filled at all. "Aren't you?"

And whatever else he was, Urian wasn't a fool. That was fear in her eyes now.

"What do you know of *gancanaghs*? I thought you claimed that faeries weren't real, Katherine."

She started shaking.

"Have you met one of us?" Urian could think of only one other: the one who destroyed his mother, the monster who was his father.

And if he hadn't had enough rage toward Irial already, he felt enough to torch the earth in this moment. Seeing Katherine look at him this way, realizing that the fear she felt must've been because she'd had some sort of encounter with his father . . . the very thought of it sickened Urian.

"I wouldn't force you." He stiffened at the insult. "I know what people think of us, and what *he* was like, but I'm nothing like my father."

She looked sick now, and Urian hated that knowing that what he was had made her look so thoroughly disgusted.

"What do you know of your father?" Kat demanded. "His *name*. What was his name? When were you born? Would you be able to describe him?"

Urian stared at her.

"My father," she started. Her voice sounded like she might weep as she added, "He was a . . . I am not human. My father was a--"

"*Gancanagh?*"

She nodded. "I never knew his real name. His *other* name. He went by Quill."

"Describe him." Urian looked at her differently, as if answers were hidden on her skin. Was she family?

"Tall. Dark. Dark hair. A laugh like . . . yours." Katherine folded her arms over her chest as if to stop from trembling. "He said there weren't many of *us*. And I know he might have had other kids and . . ."

Urian stared at her, not able to process what this meant.

"Urian?"

"Us?" he prompted. "Why do you say 'us' that way?"

"Faeries like us. *Gancanagh*." Katherine met his eyes with a pride he wasn't currently able to feel. "Addictive faery poison, you know?"

"Females of our kind are unheard of," Urian murmured, stalking closer to her. If she were family, he surely wouldn't feel such need, such raw lust.

"I'm not only fey, though." Katherine watched him, but not helplessly. She looked as if she hadn't decided if she were prey or predator.

"Where is he? When did you last see him?" Urian realized belatedly that Katherine pulled away because there was a chance they were related.

"He's dead," she answered.

And for a flicker of a moment Urian's lust burned away under rage. Had Irial died, and no one told him? Was there no way to satisfy the rage he felt toward the monster who had killed his mother and stolen both her throne from her and kept his from his own son?

Then she said, "Years ago. I barely remember him."

"You're *sure* he died? Your mother--"

"Is alive." Katherine glanced at her home. "He told her to kill him if he tried to leave because he couldn't stand the thought of her dying like that."

He looked away. "My mother was not so fortunate."

This time it was Katherine who reached out to him. Her hand gripped his wrist in what should've been a harmless gesture of comfort, but very much wasn't. And Urian dropped to his knees in the dirt.

He knelt on the ground before her, barely able to control the sheer wave of hunger that gripped him. He needed to know for sure that she wasn't family though. That was a perversion he couldn't risk.

With shaking hands, he pulled out a wallet and held it out to her. "My father's picture."

She opened it.

"Is that him?" Urian managed to say. "Is that man your father?"

Katherine looked at it. Her lips curved in a smile, and then she looked at Urian. "No. Not even close."

"Thank the gods." He wrapped his arms around her waist and pressed his face to her stomach.

When Katherine's hand dropped to his hair, Urian let

out a sound that might have embarrassed him in other circumstances. Instead, he kissed Katherine's stomach, cursing the jeans and shirt keeping her body from his.

He wasn't sure how long they'd stayed that way, but her hands were in his hair and her shirt has worked up enough that his lips brushed bare flesh. Aside from that flicker of a kiss, they were fully dressed. No proper kisses. No naked writhing. If this was how he felt before he touched her properly, he wasn't sure they'd survive being naked and entangled.

"Urian?" she said finally. "This isn't normal, right?"

And for the first time in almost a century, Urian didn't want to think about anything but this moment, this woman, this feeling of wholeness. She made him feel a kind of completion he'd only felt within Faerie.

"You need to let go of me." She let out a sighing breath. "We need to—"

"Find somewhere more private. Of course . . ." He loosened his grip, expecting her to stay close at least, thinking she must feel as lost as he did.

But Katherine was still pulling away from his embrace, and he was left staring up at her.

"No. Not that." She let out another tremulous breath. "That's just desire, not what we *need*. We should step back."

Urian came to his feet with significantly less conviction than what Katherine seemed to have. Parts of him were absolutely certain that this was, in fact, *need*, and it made movement a bit painful.

Her gaze dropped when she saw the reason he was moving slower, and he felt thoroughly guilty when he realized she was embarrassed.

"How old are you?"

"Twenty-four."

Urian felt like a monster, a twenty-four-year-old faery was little more than a child. "I'm sorry. I thought you were an adult—"

"I am! I'm *not* a child, Urian." She winced. "Not wholly fey, remember? I'm mortal enough to age like a mortal so far. . . Halfling, remember? In *mortal* years, I'm more than old enough for the thoughts you're trying not to have right now."

"I wouldn't be so sure," he muttered, but he would allow that in terms of relative age, he suspected they were closer than it might seem. The fey matured differently. And halflings were unpredictable in their aging.

Twenty-four.

In truth, she was probably slightly older than him comparatively. He'd aged entirely like the fey, but they were both adults. In that regard, they weren't far off, as despite almost a century of roaming, Urian was barely an adult in mortal maturity levels. He was, functionally, her age--but in terms of life experience, in terms of sexual explorations, he suspected they were not as close.

At all.

Carefully, he asked, "How much of a princess locked away in the tower are you, Katherine?"

She gave him a wry grin. "Enough to have fantasies that would make you stop thinking I'm too young, but no practical experience."

"None? At *all?*" Urian's mouth went dry at the thought of fantasies that a *gancanagh* in captivity would have.

Then he felt actual guilt. She deserved better than crass lust, better than him. He remembered romance. Admittedly, the first few romantic encounters he'd had were orchestrated by a well-meaning auntie who sent him to deliver this or that to half-mortals, half-fey living in Faerie.

Still, a person needed a touch of romance after a life in seclusion. He could give her that. It would be his privilege, in fact, and he would be sure to treat her as carefully as she deserved, as anyone deserved. The gift of sharing one's intimacies was unparalleled to a *gancanagh*, and the thought of sharing it with another of his kind was dizzying.

"May I kiss you, Katherine?" Urian didn't want there to be any confusion, any doubt.

Consent mattered.

They might both be the sort of faery driven by longing for touch, but that didn't mean he would fail to ask. If anything, it meant he was more concerned with being forthright.

She stared at him as if he'd spoken nonsense words, but then she licked her lips. "Why?"

"Just one kiss, Katherine. Let us begin with nothing more than that," he offered, ignoring everything. "You can't kiss mortals. Not being what we are. Haven't you ever wanted--"

"Yes, please." She stepped closer. "A kiss would be--"

And Urian had no idea what words would have followed that, because he'd pulled her into his arms and brought his lips to hers.

Chapter Thirteen

KATHERINE

Kissing Urian was not what she'd expected. Admittedly, romance novels and television weren't the best of teachers, but she hadn't expected to feel like she was swallowing shadows and lightning. She hadn't expected the universe to fill her like she might explode with the majesty of it if he moved away.

Her entire body tingled like a spark left ungrounded, looping back on itself. She clutched him, gripping his shirt like she needed to keep him from escaping.

When his hand dropped to her ass, Katherine lifted one leg to press closer.

And logic slapped her like a vat of ice water. She jerked away so hard that she fell, tumbling into the gravel and surprisingly grateful for the shock of pain that came from her fall.

"Stop."

He looked down at her. "I asked for consent."

"Yes. I gave it but . . ." She shook her head, trying to

quell her racing heart, needing to convince her body to slow down. "That wasn't a kiss."

"Oh?"

Katherine pressed her now-bleeding hand into the ground again. "It started as a kiss, but . . . I can't kiss you if that's what happens."

He squatted down so they were eye-to-eye. "What was it that happened? I thought you were happy to kiss me."

"Is it like that when you kiss other faeries? Other humans?" Katherine was fairly certain that she'd take every skill she had to fight her way to Urian's side if anyone or anything tried to separate them right now. That couldn't be normal.

"Like what?" Urian pressed.

"Like you want to consume the other person," she whispered, staring down at the ground, watching her blood make blooms in the sandy dirt. She kept her voice low as she continued, "Like lightning was building inside your body and trying to demand that you get closer. Like clothes are too much of a barrier . . ."

"And the world could burn around you and you wouldn't notice?" Urian added when her voice trailed off.

"Oh."

"Look at me." He gently touched her under the chin, tilting her head upwards until Katherine met his eyes. "In a century or so of kissing people, I've never felt that until just now. Until you."

Faeries don't lie.

This one truth was all that stood between her and complete embarrassment.

He's not lying.

"Why?"

Urian sighed. "If I knew this was what I could have, I certainly wouldn't have been able to be as patient that many days outside your window. I'd have scaled the building, begged you for a kiss . . ."

"What you could *have*?" she echoed. "I'm not a possession."

The smile he offered her was worse than the temptation of a thousand kisses. "Are you saying *you* don't want to possess *me*?"

"No . . . but normal people—"

"We are not normal people, Katherine. I am a prince without his throne, and you are the only female *gancanagh* I've ever heard of." Urian's arrogance was somehow twofold as he said the words. "A partner fit for a king."

Every rational thought she had vanished.

A *king*? Partner to a king?

Katherine scooted away from him and shook her head. "I don't know how things are in *your* world, but a kiss isn't a proposal, no matter how amazing it was."

He looked at her as if she was a strange puzzle, but he didn't step closer.

She stood, took another step backward. "We need to pause. Reconsider if--"

"If you run, I'll find you." Urian shrugged, as if such threats were casual. "You're meant for me. I'm certain of it now. I'll have to change a few of my plans, especially if you want monogamy. Do you? We can figure this out, though. We *will*. Nothing I've ever known has been so clear."

She shook her head again, crossed her arms, and protested, "You don't know me. At all."

He gestured toward the lights of the tiny downtown area. "Then join me for a meal. And I will know you."

"After one meal?" she scoffed.

"After as many meals as it takes to earn more kisses," he said. "I will romance you, Katherine, until you are as certain as I am. You *are* meant for me, and in time, you will see that."

"You're mad," she whispered. "A kiss and—"

"You changed when you met me. Woke up. You glow now when I touch you, like a beacon. Perhaps that glow is only for me. Perhaps anyone could touch you and bring that moonlight to your skin, but it's there now." He stalked closer. "And I am here. Offering myself to you. . . my beautiful *gancanagh* locked away in seclusion, filled with fantasies and longing. Tell me the thought of having someone to touch whenever you want doesn't—"

"Stop," she whispered. A rush of longing made her tremble.

He made her tremble.

She knew better, knew that lust and longing were not love, knew that everything he offered was dangerous. Wanting to learn more about her heritage wasn't the same as wanting him.

Was it?

Her heritage was a creature out of myth, the equivalent of a succubus. Not merely mortal. Not merely faery either.

Urian held her gaze. "I will not apologize for what we are. You shouldn't either."

Katherine took several breaths, trying to argue with her heart and other places more southern and demanding right now. Whatever else Urian was, he wasn't a "starter model" for a woman with no experience.

But I'm not an ordinary woman.

The glittering in his eyes and the demand in his voice

were because he felt the same hunger. He might have experience, but she was far from powerless here. He wanted her just as much as she wanted him. That knowledge hit her like a boost of adrenaline.

"So, romance me, Urian. Maybe you'll earn at least one more kiss." Katherine reached out a hand toward him, not waiting but offering.

Urian chuckled and used her hand as leverage to tug her closer. She was chest-to-chest with him.

Katherine looked up and held his gaze as she traced from his waist over his hip with her free hand. When she cupped his ass, Urian's grip on her hand tightened.

"She likes playing with danger," he murmured, words feeling like they were tangible against her lips, and she wanted to swallow them.

"Tell me something about you," she invited.

He turned his head, so his lips were against her throat. Carefully as if she were made of something delicate, he kissed her throat.

She tilted her head, angling to offer him more skin, and he chuckled before continuing to kiss her. A series of small shiver-inducing nips followed.

"He's a tease," she finally said.

Urian paused and stepped back, leaving her feeling cold without his touch. "No, love. I simply like to take my time," he promised. "*Teases* don't follow through. My kisses are promises."

Her knees felt weak as he watched her.

"If you're lucky," she taunted.

This time he laughed outright. "I intend to be very lucky, so I suppose I'd better get on with the romancing. . ."

The tension felt lighter now, not that her desires had

vanished, but as she stood with him, she realized that it was not just about touch. What she wanted was more. Romance. Ridiculous gestures. Chasing. She'd always thought of the sort of faery she was as about lust and sex. She'd reduced it to that, but now that she was hand-in-hand with Urian, she realized for perhaps the first time, that the translation of the faery into mortal explanation was limited. She wanted to charm him, seduce him, enthrall him, and she wanted to show him that the world was better because she was there. That was what a *gancanagh* was. Not simple lust.

And if he felt the same—and it very much seemed that he did—Katherine could not imagine how either of them could walk away from this unscathed. No wonder mortals died of longing. It was about so much more than touch.

She wanted him to feel as beautiful and treasured as any person ever had. How did one recover from that?

A whisper of caution, one that sounded a lot like her mother's voice, said this was a terrible idea, a *dangerous* idea. Did she want a broken heart? Did she want that aching loneliness after catching raw magic in her bare hands and losing it?

Katherine looked up at Urian. "I know next to nothing of the world of faeries, and less about romance. Show me?"

Chapter Fourteen

AISLINN

When the Hunt, now led by Chela, arrived in the park where Summer held their meetings and dances, Aislinn was reminded why they evoked such terror. She'd fought at their side. She'd seen them as allies, and yet they still filled her with the overwhelming urge to back away.

Chela's steed, Alba, shifted shapes with mood. Alba chose to express his feelings with his shape. Currently, Alba was leonine, more lion than horse, and the mane of the creature fluffed out like a cloud, half-hiding the rider.

But Chela was impossible to miss. Menace rolled off her like a perfume, and danger made her seem larger than she actually was. It was hard to tear her gaze away, but Aislinn forced herself to look at the Hunt not just the Hound that led them now.

The horses, because in some way that was the easiest way to categorize them, were not all equine in shape. There were definite horse-shaped beings, but others were more chimera-like, many animals blended into one. There was at least one dragonish shaped creature, face reptilian and enormous wings on either side of the rider. Several steeds looked like biological and mechanical hybrids, as if they were a machine's idea of a horse.

And running alongside them were creatures that seemed so horrific that Aislinn could not look upon them.

When they filled the park, their numbers seemed somehow greater than during the fight with Bananach, and still they poured into the park. A rare few of the Summer Girls twirled through the gloom and terror, as if to cure the darkness. They'd figured out how to make their binding vines into tattoos after the Summer King left, so depending on their choices, they were half ink, half vine dressed. The Hounds, a magical mix of men and women and gender fluid creatures, seemed poised for action. And at their feet were dog-like creatures which ran amongst the hooves and claws of the steeds with a grace and speed that to the average sight might look like smoke.

"Niall says you have quarry we might hunt," Chela said. She was rarely one for excess words, especially since she'd become the Gabriel after the death of her mate.

It took effort to call her by her title, but Aislinn dipped her head in respect and said, "Gabriela."

"Summer Queen."

Then Aislinn turned to the riderless steed and dipped her head to the memory of the last head of the Hunt, Gabriel. His steed rode at Chela's side. He was one of the many who stood against Bananach, and he'd died in the process.

"My uncle." Aislinn motioned to Tavish, who was blooded by the shadows that Urian had layering onto a glittering knife.

Her guard stood still as the steeds sniffed his now-healed

skin. No creature but them could find a scent on healed flesh.

Aislinn braced herself as they then stalked and prowled toward her. She held out both hands. One held the knife Urian had thrown at Tavish; the other was outstretched so that they might know her scent. Whatever else they were, they could separate her scent from the knife. They separated Tavish's scent from it. The Hunt would know her anywhere, could now find her anywhere.

To dispatch the Hunt meant letting them store her scent. Perhaps it was foolish, but she wasn't sure she was ever going to be hard to find anyhow. She was the Summer Queen. It made her fairly easy to locate.

Aislinn stayed perfectly still as the Hounds, steeds, and dogs snuffled at her. Finally, when all but Chela had done so, the leader of the Hunt herself stepped down from her steed and stalked toward Aislinn. That was the first time that Aislinn had felt raw fear trickle over her skin like the sheen of sweat.

"Do you want to run?" Chela whispered. "From now unto my death, we can find you, Aislinn. Anywhere you go, we can track."

"I didn't run when I was mortal," Aislinn whispered back. "Queens don't run."

On some level, Aislinn knew that taunting the Hunt was foolish, but she was the Summer Queen. She wasn't going to bow to anyone. Not now. Not ever. She'd surrendered her mortality, found a way to keep the man she loved, fought the embodiment of War, and was currently figuring out how to be granddaughter to the last Dark King.

Bowing was not in her.

Chela leaned close enough that she was almost touching

Aislinn's throat, and then she inhaled for what seemed like an impossible amount of time. It was frightening and weirdly erotic to have another person that close to her skin. Only Seth had been that close to her in years.

Aislinn shivered.

"You smell like your grandfather, too. No wonder Gabriel liked you." Chela's words were whispered still, but they held a wonder in them now.

She stepped back, held Aislinn's gaze, and added, "I would come for you should you ask."

Aislinn felt like there were levels of wrongness in those words—or maybe it was just the temptation she felt at the blatant offer.

"The Hunt was fond of Thelma," Chela said loudly now, once more the Gabriela, not the person. "We have followed this one's grandfather."

The Hunt was all grinning now—and there was something unsettling about horse-like, dragon-like, machine-like steeds grinning. Teeth did not always make for effective smiles, and dragon fangs definitely didn't look cheerful in ways that Aislinn found comforting.

Tavish was at Aislinn's side now, summoned by her unease.

"Steady on, Ash," he murmured.

But Aislinn was watching the start of trouble unfold in front of her. She wasn't entirely sure what to do or say, but it was akin to watching an accident in progress. She was stealing from the Dark Court, not intentionally, but would they see it that way? Would Winter think she was trying to destabilize the delicate power balance between them?

"What do you mean?" she asked the Hunt, hoping she was wrong. She knew she couldn't stop it, but she wanted to.

Chela bowed from the waist. "Your land is our land if you'll have us, Aislinn."

Aislinn swallowed, but she didn't look away when the Gabriela straightened to stare at her.

"The Hunt lives in the Dark Court," Aislinn said, not quite a question but damn near it.

"Perhaps it has, but *I* am the Gabriela. I have no need of the new Dark King's rules." Chela held Aislinn's gaze. "Would we be welcome here?"

"Yes."

"Then they will ask *you* if they might send us in the future," Chela said simply. "I do not follow any regent simply because it was that way; Hounds will make their beds where they choose."

"I am honored." Aislinn tried not to think of the trouble that was suddenly in front of her. "The Dark King—"

"Is not my concern." Chela mounted her stead. "We ride."

And in a blur of scale and fur, hooves and claws, steeds and riders, they were gone. The very air seemed to fill with sounds, as if bird and beast had paused because the Hunt was near. They were terror given form, and their departure made the world exhale again.

"What just happened?" Aislinn asked Tavish, who was grinning widely at her.

"You just accepted the Hunt to our court, Ash." He looked overjoyed.

"Yes, but how? Why?" She had theories but none of them made sense.

Or did they?

"Chela liked you," Tavish said simply. "She's not feeling

necessary in the Dark Court, and her fealty says to all and each that you are . . . more vicious."

Aislinn winced.

"You've slain War herself," Tavish added.

"Not alone."

"You have sent them after the son of the Dark King," Tavish said. "*Vicious*."

"He attacked my court," she protested. "I'm not *vi--*" The word died on her lips, a lie if ever there was one.

Faeries couldn't lie—even to themselves.

"The Hunt will go where they can best fit, and right now, Ash, that's here." Tavish waited until she looked him in the face before adding, "And if I am not mistaken, Chela finds you interesting. They already welcome Seth to their training. This was inevitable."

And to that, Aislinn had no words.

Chapter Fifteen

KATHERINE

The first place Urian took her was not the sort of place she expected. He led her to a parking lot, not to a dinner or a romantic get-away or any such place. He had a car, seemingly modified for their kind. To her eyes, it appeared to be a cherry red 1970-something Chevy Chevelle. Wide white stripes across the hood, a white roof, and whitewall tires. There was not a scratch anywhere, making the car look as if it was fresh off a showroom, despite being over fifty years old.

"Wow." She reached out as if to touch the car, but suddenly, she had the strange suspicion that it was somehow alive. There was no motion, but as she'd gotten closer, she thought the car was breathing.

"She's friendly," Urian murmured, petting a hand over the roof, and Katherine wasn't certain whether he was speaking to her or the car.

"Where are we going?" she hesitated, unable to figure out how or why the car seemed alive.

"I want you to see what we can be," Urian said, still not very helpfully.

"And that takes a car?"

"Yes." He opened the door, pausing to pet the side of the vehicle. "Your chariot."

She slid into beautiful deep red leather seats with white trim. Her family wasn't financially desperate, but her mother would never agree to a car like this. It practically screamed "look at me." Hiding meant that ostentatious everything was forbidden, and sometimes what Katherine missed most was her father's bolder-than-brass attitude. He was in your face, loud, unashamed.

Maybe it's a gancanagh thing.

Katherine glanced over at Urian. "Are we all like this?"

He shot her a grin. "Devastatingly handsome? Irresistible?"

She laughed. "Big ego . . ."

"Yes. To all of it." Urian still looked happy, but he sounded more serious. "Once, a very long time before either of us existed, there were faeries—*gancanangh* and leannan-sidhe—who were seducers." He paused and glanced at her before resuming his storyteller voice. "We were made to destroy mortals. Our skin irresistible, our touch addictive, and so we go through this world alone. We are deadly to them, and they want us more than life."

"But . . . the folklore . . . and my mother. Not *all* mortals die." Katherine looked at him, folding her hands into fists. The more he spoke in that tone--that lifting and falling, like tides luring her into a dangerous sea—the more she felt caught in the undertow.

He reached out and stroked the back of her hand, one

thumb gliding over her knuckles and across the thin skin of her hand. That was it. One touch.

Katherine trembled.

"Shall I seduce you?" he asked, lightly as if he was talking about the weather. And maybe that was part of being what he was. Maybe he wasn't lying when he said the kiss they'd shared was powerful, but that didn't mean that he was anything more than a fleeting experience.

Do I want him to be?

That was the question she couldn't answer. She felt more alive since meeting him, but maybe that would be the case with any faery she talked to and longed to touch. Maybe she was simply becoming more faery.

"Where are we going?" she asked, pulling her hand away from him and folding it in her lap.

He looked away from the road, staring at her and pointedly not paying any attention to driving.

"Not immortal, pretty boy. How about you put your eyes on the road?" Katherine squirmed, hoping it wasn't obvious.

"Close your eyes for several heartbeats, and then when you open them, *look* at the car." He reached out like he would touch her eyelids.

Katherine flinched away, raising one hand to block him.

"Count to six," he ordered. "Eyes closed."

Despite her doubts, she did so, silently counting out each number. Then she opened her eyes and stared at the car.

"This is . . . not a car," she whispered.

The creature—for that's what it was—was some sort of wild animal that was wearing the idea of a car, but it was not a machine. It was fully and completely alive. Katherine could feel a heartbeat not her own, thumping faster than hers did even when afraid.

"What is she?" Katherine asked, because she recalled him referring to the car-creature as "she."

Urian shrugged. "A friend."

When Katherine made a face, he added, "She came to me as a small sheeplike creature. Then as an alligator. Often, these days, she is a horse. When I need to travel with a passenger or in mortal spaces, she is a car."

"What's her name?"

"I have no idea." Urian shrugged. "She does not speak in that way."

It hit Katherine then that there was something disconcerting in the idea of a car that was not a car, but a creature. As a car, there was a roof overhead, and she'd entered through a door.

"I feel like I climbed into her mouth or something," Katherine whispered.

The radio switched on and a snippet of a song played: "You are safe in my arms."

Katherine startled. Her imagination sparked. She could picture some strange undefinable creature running along the narrow road, carrying passengers in her massive arms.

"She doesn't talk often," Urian murmured. "She must like you."

Katherine patted the seat, hoping what she was petting was an arm or shoulder. "I don't know what's where here, so please forgive me if this is not okay."

The radio clicked on to play a laugh track.

And Katherine smiled at the strangeness of it all.

Urian and Katherine drifted toward silence as the car travelled faster and faster.

"Do you get a lot of speeding tickets?" she finally asked. The world outside blurred a bit, as the creature moved at speeds that were somewhere between high-speed trains and airplanes.

"Faery, love. We can be invisible to the mortal eye," Urian teased. "Glamours. I could've watched you, unseen to every eye in that building but *you* for eternity. You could stalk me, unseen by most everyone in this state."

Katherine nodded. "I've never . . . I mean . . . I'm not sure *how*."

"I'll teach you," Urian promised.

And despite good sense, she teased, "Well, that wasn't *precisely* the first lesson I was seeking from you, but we can add it to the list . . ."

Urian's gaze was heated as he glanced her way. "Careful, Katherine. You taunt too much and—"

"I trust you. You already said you needed consent for a simple kiss," she reminded him. Then, smiling, she held his gaze a moment longer than comfortable, before adding, "And I like the way you're looking at me right now."

"How's that?"

"Like you're the one being seduced," she admitted.

Chapter Sixteen

URIAN

Nearly an hour later, they walked along a trail, deeper into a pine forest. Urian's pulse was still thrumming faster than he'd expected. He was not expecting to meet a female of his kind, and while he could appreciate the company of men, he wasn't drawn as much in that direction.

I am not like my father.

News of the former Dark King's long romance with the current Dark King—a romance that predated Irial's time with Urian's mother—was reason enough to avoid any other gancanaghs.

I am nothing like him. The thought that the mere presence of another *gancanagh* was enough to make a person desperate seemed foolish. Urian assumed that his father was simply weak.

But, unfortunately, Urian's reaction to Katherine meant that he did share this trait with his father—and he hated the reality that he felt pulled to *gancanagh*s or sometimes to mortals. It was as if Urian lacked self-control. He couldn't accept that possibility, couldn't allow himself to believe it because it would mean he was no better than the monster who was his father,

I am better than him.

But how was a man to define himself in opposition to a faery who had found favor with the High Queen, seduced a mortal destined for the Summer King, and defeated death to become the embodiment of Chaos?

"Are you okay?" Katherine asked, breaking the silence between them.

Urian took her hand in his. "May I?"

She drew a sharp breath, closed her eyes, and then whispered, "Yes."

Of course, Urian felt the same spark of longing she was wrestling with—more than with any person he'd ever touched before—but he was prepared for it. Katherine was an innocent.

"Would you like me to put my gloves on?" he offered. "No direct skin contact . . .?"

"No. I want this. I just . . ." She shivered. "I need a minute."

They stood there, hand-in-hand, birds overhead, soft forest floor under their feet. And it was everything he could want in this instant.

Carefully he teased, "Perhaps, we are seducing each other . . ."

"Yes," she answered, not bothering to dissemble as most faeries did. It was a peculiar thing: she either lied or was honest. There was nothing in the middle with Katherine. Most fey lied by clever twists of words, misdirection, and evasion. He *could* lie, but it was a sort of pain that made him wonder if death might be kinder.

Katherine was an anomaly in so very many ways.

Mine, his heart insisted.

However, it was not only his heart that was invested here. Urian's skin felt flush with desire at the mere touch of her bare skin in his hand.

Then, as if his wants were in her mind too, or perhaps they had the same need, Katherine stepped so she was facing him.

"One minute," she said. "I need one minute."

He stared down at her. "I am not rushing you . . ."

His words faded as she reached up with her free hand and stroked his cheek. Just a thumb over the skin on his cheek as he had done with her hand on the trip here, but that one touch made him hold his breath.

"One minute?" he asked. "To gain self-control?"

Her hand slid back so she was cupping the side of his head, tilting him toward her, directing her, and Urian's lips parted in surprise.

"To seduce you the way you are seducing me.

"Oh . . ."

"Let me seduce you, Urian," she whispered. "Don't move."

Then her lips ghosted over his: fleeting, not even a full kiss. Her breath passed over his throat, under the line of his jaw and toward his ear. And after a soft exhale that was more sigh than word, she caught his earlobe between her teeth for the flicker of a moment.

Katherine whispered, "Thank you."

Urian was shaken—not only from not moving as she'd asked of him, but from the thrill of someone wanting to seduce *him*, not simply wanting to be seduced by him.

"That helps," she said mildly as she started to walk,

pulling him in her wake as their hands were still entwined. "Knowing you'll give me control."

"Yes, please," he murmured--because what else could he possibly say?

She laughed, sounding free and joyous, and he found he liked that as much as her touches.

"Part of learning is practice, right?" she quipped.

"Happy to be of service." Urian's smile was wider than he'd felt in all of his adult life, and he thought briefly that perhaps toppling thrones wasn't really as much of a priority as he'd believed.

Maybe being here--with this woman, in this place—was enough.

"Come on," he said. "Places to see. People to meet. Woman to impress . . ."

She laughed again as she let him take the lead toward the hot springs where he liked to escape. Later, there would be a gathering of faeries and halflings like them, who gathered in the woods in the northeast corner of New Mexico.

By the time they'd woven themselves along the trail to the hot springs, Urian had decided to tell her the plan.

"There are others like us who will be here tonight," he said.

"Halflings?"

"Faeries, some of dual parentage and some not," he clarified. "I thought you might want to meet people other than me."

"Do I need gloves?" Katherine looked up at him, and he was stricken by how much kinder she was. Not merely hungry. Not filled with rage. She worried that her touch would cause trouble.

"You won't *hurt* anyone by touching them," he hedged.

"But . . .?"

"But they'll likely be aroused to some degree," Urian paused, weighing his words before adding, "You are uncontrolled in a way that will change with time. Your every need is ready to be met, and while that is true, you will be alluring. It will not hurt them, but I would prefer if you tried not to touch bare skin."

"Because you want to be the one to quench that need?" Katherine's voice was light, and she smiled.

Urian exhaled in relief. "No. Obviously, I *do*, but who has that fortune is your choice. I would simply rather you do not yet see me in the sort of violence I would be prone towards if you were in peril."

She stared at him for a long moment. "Are you often violent?"

"I can be." Urian looked at her unflinchingly. "Come with me, and let me have lightness tonight, and tomorrow I will tell you all my flaws."

"We need all day to list them?" she teased, smile wavering apprehensively but still there.

"No." He tugged her hand so that they were walking again.

A few moments later, they stood at the edge of a hot spring. The state was dotted with them, but this one was hidden. Used only by faeries, it was tucked in a natural dip in a hillside, so that it looked like a great hand had carved a hole in the earth. About the size of a small swimming pool, tiny lake, or enormous pond, the hot spring in front of them would easily fit several dozen people at once.

Urian had layered "mortals stay away" magic over the whole area so that his kind had this slice of nature to themselves. It was a skill his auntie had taught him. This and hiding his true heritage were the greatest tools he'd had in his arsenal of tricks.

"I don't have a suit," she said.

"Do you need one?"

"I'm not having sex with you today," she rebutted.

"Noted." He grinned. "Not *today*."

She laughed. "No guarantees about other days either, but definitely not today."

"Define 'sex,' Katherine of Miller." Urian watched the pulse in her throat thrum. "Does touching your hand constitute sex? Kissing? What are the rules here? Or do you simply mean *intercourse*?"

She was breathy as she said, "That last one."

"So I will get another kiss?" He watched her lips part.

Katherine nodded silently.

"That is more than enough." He wanted more, and she did too, but there was time enough. They could take their seduction slowly.

As Urian turned his back, he added, "I will give you privacy to slip into the water if you want. There's room in the pool, and there are shadows to hide any glimpses of your bare self."

"And if I want to enjoy the hot spring without you?" she asked.

"Then I will guard your privacy." Urian wanted her to be happy in a way that was foreign to him, and this hot spring was relaxing to him. He admitted, "I merely want you to enjoy a place that I love. And if that means that I stand here with my back to you, and we speak while you relax, it is enough."

Chapter Seventeen

KATHERINE

There was something delicious about control, and something even more so about Urian. He made her feel like breaking every rule she thought she had to live by--rules not only about who she was, but about what options she had.

Other faeries are going to be here tonight.

That ought to make her feel afraid. Instead, she felt like she knew she would be safe just because he'd be at her side.

"Katherine?" Urian's back was to her still, and she found herself feeling bold in ways that felt scandalous. She was twenty-four, not a child. She knew she aged differently because she wasn't entirely human, but there was no doubt in her mind that she was beyond ready for the promises he was holding out to her.

She kicked off her shoes. "Stripping."

"Wonderful idea." He paused, as if listening. "May I join you?"

"In the water? Not yet." She stepped closer to him, pulling her shirt off and handing it to him, reaching one bare arm around him. "Hold this?"

He took her shirt.

"And this?" She unfastened her bra and held it to him.

Again, mutely, he took the piece of clothing.

Pressing closer, she whispered, "Don't turn around."

Urian nodded.

Katherine unbuttoned her jeans, slid out of them. "I'm wearing only my panties, but I think . . . I think I'll keep those on, Urian."

"Because . . .?" His voice was harsher, deeper now, and Katherine felt a thrill that it was because of her.

She put a hand on both of his shoulders, leaning into him. "Because I'm not ready to be naked with you. Yet."

He reached up to hold her closer to him, so her nearly-naked body was pressed against his back. "I'll be waiting."

"Anxiously?" She reached out and caught his chin, turning him so he was looking at her face.

He didn't resist. "Eagerly."

"Good." She grinned. "Am I terrible if I ask you to get in the hot spring with me?"

"Not at all," Urian assured her. "Would you like me to wait until you're in the water, hidden from my view?"

She paused. Being exposed to that shadowed gaze felt more like throwing fuel on a carefully burning fire than she was ready for, but she wanted to be fair, too. "Kind of . . . but I want to see you."

He swallowed audibly before asking, "Explain?"

"Naked. I want to see you." Her voice trembled, but she wasn't going to hide her interest. She was what she was, and that was a faery that was born to incite lust. Whatever mortal side she'd had sheltering her seemed to have fled when she met Urian.

When he didn't speak, she added, "I don't have half the

control I did before I met you, Urian. I thought . . . I thought I was more mortal than not, but right now . . ."

"Tell me when to turn around," was all he said. He brushed a kiss over her knuckles and released her hand.

Katherine took one step away from him, before turning and walking to the hot springs. She slid into the hot water with a sigh that was as much for the water as the glimpse she had of Urian's now-naked back. A back ought not be that alluring, but she fisted her hands to resist the urge to touch, to trace every line of muscle on the dark skin that he'd exposed.

"Urian?"

She heard his jeans buttons slipping free, louder than any sound should be in a forest. Maybe she only imagined the sound because she could see that his hands were at his waist.

"Would you turn around?" She stood in the hot water, it was hip high, so the only part of her that was exposed was from her waist up.

Silently, he turned, gaze on her body seeming as tangible as a touch. He watched her as he finished unfastening his jeans and slid them to the ground.

"Tell me I'm not selfish?" she half-whispered, half begged.

"You aren't." He smiled so that she couldn't doubt him, even if he could lie. "Wanting isn't selfish."

"What if I want you to keep stripping? I still have my--"

"Not selfish." He removed the last piece of clothing, standing naked before her. "Shall I stay right here, Katherine? Let you have both your look and your space?"

She swallowed. Nothing had prepared her for Urian, no amount of internet surfing or movies that she could only watch in the dark with her door locked and headphones on.

He was there, naked and beautiful, and clearly as excited as she felt.

"What do you want, Katherine?" He trailed a hand over his stomach and downward, stopping just shy of touching himself. "Do you want me to stand here naked and silent? Do you want to watch me touch—"

"Join me in the spring."

In a sliver of a moment, he was slipping into the hot water, hiding half his body from her gaze, but she couldn't cross every line at once. Watching him touch himself sounded more tempting than anything ought to be, but it also sounded like it might be more than she thought any "first date" ought to be.

"What thoughts cloud your eyes?" he asked.

"Embarrassment . . .?" she admitted.

And Urian frowned. "Why? For liking the look of me? For wanting to look? For letting me see your lovely skin? For driving me mad with the urge to touch you?"

"No. Maybe? I don't even know. We just met." She sunk deeper into the water, so only the tops of her shoulders were exposed. "I don't understand. I've met so many people in so many states, and I've never flashed my breasts at *any* of them."

"Poor things. They ought to weep at their loss," Urian murmured. "I feel blessed."

Katherine laughed. "Weirdo."

He shrugged, making even that look sexy. "We aren't mortals, Katherine. Never forget that. But . . . we aren't simply fey either. *Gancanaghs* are rare. A female one? I've never even heard whispers of such a thing."

"But . . . I don't want to be . . ." She struggled to find the words.

A lifetime of mortal-only life was hard to overcome in a moment. Worse still, she couldn't stop hearing her mother's warnings that the fey were dangerous, that she might be dangerous, that a part of what she was could only ever be poison.

"Be what?"

"I'm not even sure," she admitted. "I'm dangerous. Touching me is *deadly*."

"Not to me." Urian stayed at a distance, not exactly on the opposite side of the pool, but not close enough to touch, not crowding her.

"*You're* dangerous," she objected.

"Not to you." He smiled at her. "In all the world, Katherine, I've never met anyone else who was less in danger from me. You are what I am. If there is anything dangerous here, it's to both of us equally."

She nodded.

"And Katherine?"

She lifted her gaze to him.

"Nothing you want of me is a reason for embarrassment." He kept his voice pitched low. "I've spent over a century in this world. I've done things . . . tried things . . . and they are far more wicked than letting a beautiful woman look at my body."

"What if I want to do more than look?" she whispered, looking down in embarrassment at how bold she was being, and even though she stayed far away from him, she could tell by the shadows in his eyes that he heard each word clearly.

He held open his arms, inviting. "All yours, Katherine. I said I wanted to show you what we are."

"I don't want to use you . . ." she admitted. "And I'm not ready for . . . all the things I want. I don't want to get you all"

—she forced herself to meet his heated gaze—"aroused and then . . . make a bad decision."

Katherine was relieved that he didn't laugh. It seemed awkward as hell to talk about these things, but she also had thought about this potential situation man of times late at night since she'd met him.

"I trust you, and I ask that you trust me when I say that being aroused isn't a bad thing. At all. You are not the only *gancanagh* who has spent nights alone with fantasies and a hand."

She forced herself not to look away.

"I have imagined *you* touching me." He smiled encouragingly. "Today, I give you my oath, Katherine of Miller. I will not have intercourse with you, and you are free to touch me until your heart is content."

She stilled at the fact that he had just given her a vow, felt the weight of it as he said the words.

"And Katherine?"

She waited with her pulse thumping like a drum.

"All I'm swearing is no intercourse," he clarified. "If there's anything else sexual you want of me, say the word."

She nodded and treaded water toward him. "I want you *not* to touch me right now. Can you . . ."

Her words trailed off as smoke coalesced at his wrists, like manacles holding his wrists to the stones of the hot springs.

"At your mercy, Katherine." Urian watched her with more predator than prey in his gaze. "Until you say the words, these arms are bound."

Chapter Eighteen

AISLINN

Of all the people Aislinn expected to find at her doorstep, her almost-lover, the former Summer King was the last she expected.

"Ash." Keenan looked different now. No less regal, but he certainly was not glowing as Summer Court faeries tended to do. He was the son of the last Winter Queen, who was killed by them a bit over five years ago.

My co-murderer.

In fairness, the last Winter Queen had attacked both Seth, Aislinn's beloved, and Donia, the current Winter Queen who had been Keenan's beloved for a century. It was self-defense, as well as in defense of those whom Beira had attacked.

Murder and sharing the throne of the Summer Court had left them with an awkward bond.

"Where is Donia?" Aislinn prompted, leading Keenan away from the loft that had been his home, then their shared home. She always felt strangely awkward there with him.

"We thought it might be easier if I spoke to you informally," Keenan said, offering her his arm in a way that was habitual and gentlemanly.

Aislinn rested her hand in the fold of his arm, gently. Summer and Winter had an affinity, but the two of them also had a history.

The last person to kiss me other than Seth.

"So we are meeting as friends," she teased. "Pretending this is not business or rumors that bring you to my doorstep?"

"Can we not be friends?" Keenan led her toward the center of town, away from the gossiping member of the Summer Court.

"Were we ever truly?" Aislinn kept pace, focusing on her emotions and her sunlight.

Keenan, like Donia, was filled with the ice of winter. Deadly to her if he were stronger, but he was alone. Half of Winter. So she was the danger here, and they both knew it. He came alone, so as not to be a threat.

Politics, not real friendship. They weren't at odds, but they weren't close.

"I think of you as a friend," Keenan murmured, surprising them both when the direct words fell easily from his lips. "Donia does, as well. This is why I am asking you directly—as a friend—why the Dark visits your house of late."

Aislinn sighed, wondering how much to share, wondering what he already knew. Politics were easier after several years of practice, but there was a chasm between her and Keenan. He was raised to this, spent nine centuries dealing with it, and she had . . . not even a decade of experience.

"Ash?" Keenan prompted, still strolling at her side as if they were merely nobles in another era.

"Once upon a time," she began, "there was a woman in New Orleans called Thelma Foy. She was your destined queen, Keenan."

He stilled briefly, a misstep that could have been a stumble.

"I never found Thelma Foy," he said mildly. "I knew of her, of course. Niall had found her, but . . . I never found her."

"True." Aislinn led him to a bench alongside a street where a coffee shop had recently opened. "Do you want to know why? It might be better not to know, Keenan. I say this as a friend and . . ." Her words drifted away, as if she was not sure how to finish that statement.

Keenan waited. A thin line of frost outlined his frost steps, but it did not touch her. He was as capable with ice as he had been with sunlight. She wasn't sure how he'd dealt with both sides of himself, and in a secret thought she wasn't eager to share, she wondered if his limitations as Summer King were, in part, because he'd kept that sliver of ice in his heart all those years.

For a moment, Aislinn watched several faeries watching them, whispering and wondering. She smiled at them with more than a bit of bared teeth and waited for them to scurry away.

"Ash?"

The Summer Queen sighed louder. "Thelma was my great-grandmother, Keenan. You pursued her. You pursued my mother. Do you see the pattern?"

The former Summer King stared at her, frost pluming

from his lips as he weighed that detail. He looked irritated, but she wasn't sure if it was at her or himself.

"My missing queen was always one of the women in your family," he said quietly, after several exhaled clouds of frosty air.

"Women *or* men," she amended.

"I . . . don't, that is, I'm not like Irial and Niall in that regard," Keenan said, a bit awkwardly.

"I know. That doesn't make it less true." Aislinn wasn't sure if that was enough reason to satisfy his questions, if this sliver of truth-telling would send him away, thinking she had shared everything. She couldn't exactly *lie* about it, and her skills of deception were not as practiced as Keenan's.

He has, of course, seduced dozens of young women, stolen their mortality. It created a level of skill she could not match.

"So the Dark has come to reveal this to you because . . .?" Keenan shifted so he could stare into her face. Snowflakes drifted behind his eyes, and the Summer Queen wondered how terrible he could be if angered. A certainty came over her that a rage-fueled Winter King would be devastating. He was, after all, the child of two faeries who nearly destroyed the world as a result of their twisted love affair.

She'd seen Keenan when he was willing to let the world die for love of Donia.

She'd felt his rage when he breathed sunlight into his mother and took her life, literally burning her to death with sunlight.

She'd seen his passion when he gambled his throne for Aislinn's promise to try to love him.

The former Summer King was a man who had been born of Summer and Winter's deadly love. He was a man who was raised in one court, knowing he would rule the opposing court, a man who sacrificed his faery nature for love and then sought a curse in order to return to life as a faery. Underestimating him was dangerous—but so was telling him the whole truth at once. Winter could be as deadly as summer.

"The Dark Court knows why *you* couldn't find Thelma," she hedged.

"Did they kill her?"

Aislinn stared at him, not sure how he could so obviously misunderstand another regent. In her few years as a faery queen, she'd strived to understand the courts, to study them to better know how to negotiate with them, to better destroy them if need be. Keenan saw only ugliness when he looked at Irial--and now Niall.

Would he see her differently knowing what he was about to discover?

"*Kill* her?" Aislinn echoed. "You think Irial killed Thelma?"

"Yes, did Irial kill or give the order to kill the woman to stop—"

"No, Keenan, he did not kill my great-grandmother." Aislinn glared at him, temper leaking in bright rays of sunlight. "He fell in love with her. He followed her to Faerie, and he fathered two children with her."

Keenan laughed. "You've figured out a way around the no-lies rules! Joking. It's all in the tone and—"

"No. Irial is my great-grandfather," she said bluntly. "Grams is his daughter. *Her* mother was Thelma. My grandmother has lived so long because she is not fully human. She's the daughter of a king, in fact. I am the great-granddaughter of the last Dark King."

Keenan's mouth opened and closed, silently trying to say

words that did not come. So Aislinn figured she'd get to the current concern while he was dumb-founded.

"Irial had a second child with Thelma, Keenan. A son." Aislinn crossed her arms. The mere thought of Urian angered her, and she had to focus. "My great-uncle. Urian came to my door, fueled by rage, insisting that he was the heir to *my* throne."

Keenan's mouth closed. Whatever else he was, he was also practiced in hiding his emotions. He watched her from behind emotionless eyes—and after so many dealings with the Dark Court, she found that she hated it. There was no guessing with Irial, and she rather liked that.

I am, after all, Summer, which isn't known for subtlety.

"Urian stabbed Tavish. Well, he aimed for Siobhan, but . . ." She looked away. Rage wasn't useful in this moment, but she was having difficulty quieting the feeling. Urian had threatened what was hers, people who were hers to protect and guide. Family or not, he would suffer for such arrogance.

"Are they uninjured?" Keenan asked carefully.

Aislinn nodded, swallowed hard against the remembered fear, and assured him, "They are fine now. Together, in fact, romantically. I healed Tavish . . . and you know how sunlight is." She shrugged, unable to forget that he had taught her that detail.

"Feeling drunk and forgetting his propriety for a moment," Keenan surmised with a light chuckle.

"And Niall? How did the Dark respond to—"

"I cannot speak for another court," she interrupted. "I can only share what was related to me, not to those things beyond my involvement. I will say that Irial and Niall both came to my home at my request. You could speak to Niall.

Ask him. Tell him you know of my, err, great-grandfather's relationship with Thelma and of his tie to me."

This time, it was Keenan who sighed. The current Dark King had more than a few points of contention with the former Summer King. Near-eternal lives, secrets, and deceits made for complicated relationships.

Unfortunately, Aislinn was already discovering that reality as she sat with her almost-an-ex. They weren't *really* ex-lovers, as they never crossed that line for real, but they were more than friends. It, thankfully, wasn't as complicated as the relationship between Keenan and the Dark King who had stolen Keenan's intended lover—her great-grandmother.

She paused as the weirdness hit her.

"Sort of creepy that you wanted to romance my great-gram, *and* my mother, *and me* . . ." she murmured.

He had the grace to look a little sheepish, but then he asked, "Are there things you wouldn't do for your court, Aislinn?"

"Not that I've discovered."

For several moments, Keenan and Aislinn sat together, watching faeries and mortals pass. The only hint of the Winter Court consort's upset was the growing stretch of ice from under his feet. He said nothing more, simply waited.

Aislinn, in a blink, melted the sheet of ice that was stretching toward the street where cars would be in danger if it were to reach under their tires. Icy patches were no longer common year-round, not since the Winter and Summer courts were again balanced.

"And is there more I ought to know of your great-uncle?" Keenan finally asked.

"Urian is angry." Aislinn stood, seeing Tavish approaching. She paused, met Keenan's gaze and added, "But then again, so am I. I'll handle it—or the Dark will if Urian challenges them. I cannot imagine Niall dealing with that any better than I did."

"I suppose it depends on Irial's involvement," Keenan mused. "Even apart, they were never truly able to let go. If this is Irial's son . . ."

"Urian is filled with rage, Keenan. He's not sending handmade Father's Day cards or anything."

Keenan paused, as if deciding what secrets he would share. Then he said, "When Niall was injured, Irial would slip into whatever home we had then, heal Niall, and vanish. Niall never knew."

Aislinn stared.

"Niall was never truly Summer Court. I couldn't . . . sunlight was not what he needed, so Irial came. Every. Time." Keenan shook his head, as if it was confusing. "He's a monster, but Irial would do anything for love. He made a mistake with Niall long before I was born, but he spent literal centuries making repairs."

"Irial isn't the Dark King," Aislinn said. "And neither Niall nor I have that same trait. Urian made a mistake challenging me."

Then she turned and walked away. Some inkling of mistrust made her unwilling to mention the Wild Hunt—or perhaps that was simply politics. Why mention things before it was time?

Perhaps, Aislinn admitted to herself as she walked away to join Seth, *I simply don't want to admit that I am the queen, the regent, the creature so vicious that they have chosen to leave the Dark Court for me.*

After a childhood of knowing that the creatures most deadly of all the fey were those that dwelled in the Dark

Court, what was she to do with knowing that the blood of the Dark Court was hers? What did it mean that she was party to the death of not one but two ancient faeries? She held the last Winter Queen as Keenan killed her, and she entombed Bananach, the embodiment of War, in boiling earth and vine as Niall stabbed her.

Perhaps, Aislinn admitted, *the Wild Hunt sees me more truly than most do.*

Chapter Nineteen

KATHERINE

Nothing in her short life had prepared her to have a captive faery under her hands in a secreted hot spring. Honestly, Katherine wasn't sure anyone could be prepared for this.

She'd lost track of time as she explored the lines of Urian's naked body, and true to his word, he remained bound. Time slid past, the sun falling closer and closer to the horizon.

When he caught her looking at the sky again, Urian whispered, "We have until the moon rises, Katherine. An hour still. . ."

She looked back at him.

"Do you tire of your exploration already?" he teased, lowering his head so his forehead was pressed against hers.

"No."

"After today, I think you could recognize this body as mine with your eyes closed," he murmured. Then, before she could think to ask if he minded, he added, "I am the luckiest creature in either world right now. You know that, I hope."

Her hands trailed over his sides and to the tempting length between his legs.

Urian's breath was yet again a shuddering gasping noise that made her feel powerful. "This is what you are. What I am."

"And if I want more than I have taken so f—"

"Not *taken*," he interjected. "Accepted, Katherine. You accepted what I give freely, my body to your needs."

She was quiet a moment, enjoying the way he strained toward her, relishing the noises he made. There was no need to ask if she was mistaken. After several hours, she could read him as surely as any book in her true language. Katherine was not so foolish as to think she understood all bodies, even all men, but she was certain that she was reading this man correctly.

"May I . . .?"

"Yes. Whatever the question, yes." Urian gasped. After hours of touching him, this was the first time she wasn't pausing to ask questions first. It was the first time she was certain she wanted to see him throw his head back in the shuddering pleasure that she *knew* could give him.

Carefully, Katherine eased closer, straddling him. Only the thin material of her underwear kept him from sliding inside her body. She'd moved over him this way earlier, testing, trying new things, and he'd stayed perfectly still at her request.

"If I asked you to unbind your hands, to hold me—"

"Yes," he said.

"And if I ask you to touch me . . .?" She kissed the side of his throat again. "Would you?"

The noise he made was more groan than word, but she heard, "Please" between the sounds all the same.

"Are you asking?" he asked a moment later.

"Touch me, Urian."

"Where?" He met her gaze, and his jaw was clenched as he waited for the answer.

"Anywhere? Everywhere?"

The smoky bonds that held his wrists vanished, and briefly she realized that he could have removed them at any point. They were for her comfort, not his.

Then his hands caught her hips under the water, and he pulled her closer. Her lips parted on a sound she couldn't even name, and his mouth covered hers. The kisses, fleeting and lingering, that she'd given him were nothing compared to his mastery over her.

When he paused, he asked, "Tell me what *you* like, Katherine. I've answered your questions. Will you do the same?"

"You. I like you," she murmured.

He chuckled. "Thank the gods."

Then the hands on her hips shifted, and his thumbs were between her thighs. He traced the ribboned edge of her panties, watching her face as he did so. He didn't go any further than that.

"Under the fabric or over it?" was all he said.

"Yes." She didn't blush, didn't look away. "Please? No one else has ever touched my body there . . . only me."

He groaned. "Someday, I would love to see that, but right now . . . kneel over me."

She moved, and he parted his legs, bracing his back against the rock side of the hot spring, so he was a table to support her.

"I don't want to ignore your needs," she whispered as she tried to stroke him, too.

This time, the dark laugh that slipped between Urian's lips made her whimper. "*This* is my need. Trust me. Put your hands on the side of the wall, Katherine."

And maybe it was the falling night, or the fear that this would be unfinished before the faeries arrived here, or maybe it was the act of surrendering the control she'd been holding over him for hours, but Katherine obeyed without question.

"Like this?" He stroked her gently over her remaining clothing, and she gasped.

Then he moved the material to the side, and his fingers slid inside her body. "Or like this?"

She leaned backwards, bowing her body, arching into his touch.

And Urian completed the lesson she'd asked for when she'd asked to touch him. A worrying voice asked her how she would ever let go of him when this fling passed, but that voice was drowned by the waves of pleasure that were making her writhe and whimper under his touch.

If not for the desperate noises he was also making—and had been making for hours--she might feel embarrassed.

"This is what we are," Urian told her, staring at her as she trembled from the first orgasm anyone had given her. "Days, and months, and years of this, Katherine. I can give that to you."

She bit her lip to keep promises from escaping.

"My queen, my everything," he murmured, as he slid her closer to his body. "Your clothes are between us, love. May I touch you *this* way? Not intercourse. That was your rule . . ."

As he spoke, she felt the length she had held in her hand nestled between her legs, firm against her silk-covered skin, pressing exactly where she was still throbbing with desire.

"Yes."

And he began to move, hands on her hips.

After a moment, she ordered, "Step forward."

Urian obeyed as easily as she had obeyed him, and Katherine locked her ankles behind him. No passive partner, Katherine moved as she needed, her body finding the rhythm of this dance as easily as every other thing that day.

"Made for me," he whispered against her mouth.

Afterward, Katherine watched Urian step out of the hot spring, naked and dripping. The thought that this was her day, her life right now, seemed so far from everything before him that she pinched her own arm.

He caught her. "Still awake, love?"

"You aren't . . . this . . ." She shook her head. "I fear I've lost half my words, and all my sense."

He reached out a hand to help her out of the pool. "You aren't alone in feeling thus."

It felt foolish, but she was grateful when he turned his back to dress.

Katherine slid her last piece of clothing off, standing completely naked in the forest with an equally naked Urian, and she couldn't suppress a flicker of a thought that there was no need to stop where they had.

Why pause?

Why meet other people?

Why not find a private place and—

"The guests will arrive soon," Urian said mildly, as if he could hear her thoughts.

"You're not a mind reader, are you?" She kept her voice teasing, despite her flash of worry. "Turn around, please?"

He did, and his gaze slid over her like lightning dancing on her skin. "No mind reading, love. Not at all. At least not *your* mind. That was my way of reminding myself that we must leave, or you must cover your beautiful self. I have no compunction about an audience, but I thought . . ." He shrugged. "Perhaps not now."

"Or ever." Katherine rolled her eyes.

He shrugged again. "As you say. I'm flexible on the particulars as long as I'm able to be with you."

Then he pulled his jeans on, as she stood watching him in appreciation. Katherine couldn't say whether it was because of the godlike shape of his body or if it was some primal connection because they were both *gancanaghs*, but she had to look away before the compulsion to touch him overrode sense.

"Hey?" He held out her clothes. "You aren't alone in the thoughts you have."

She slipped her jeans on sans underwear. Putting jeans on *over* wet panties seemed like a terrible idea. "I hadn't thought this through when I stepped into the spring with those on."

"Armor," he said simply. "You needed them."

"And you in bonds?" she said in an equally light voice.

Urian caught her hand and lifted it to his lips. "Whatever rules mean that you are in my arms are *exactly* the right ones, love. Intimacy requires comfort. Trust. Not simply two—or more—bodies touching. This is your journey, and I am honored to be a part of it."

She nodded.

"And I hope, selfishly or not, that I will get to stay at your side," he added.

"Because I'm a *gancanagh* and—"

"Because you are *mine*," he interrupted. "And because I am *yours*."

Chapter Twenty

URIAN

Urian had no compunction at calling himself an exiled prince, but he had rarely felt so regal as he did with Katherine at his side. She was on his arm, dressed in all but her underwear, which he'd put in his pocket. That thought was somehow more distracting than it seemed like it ought to be. How was he to overthrow kings and queens if he couldn't stop wishing everyone and everything would vanish? He wanted her, only her, and damn his plans and dreams.

Quietly, he said, "Those are thistle fey."

She nodded. "I've seen them before."

One of the dark fey's thistle-covered hands brushed too close to her, drawing blood from her wrist, and Urian lashed out with a sharp-edged shadow.

Blood dripped to the ground like a punctuation of his, "Do not touch her."

"Sorry, prince."

There were already almost fifty faeries in the wood, and somehow it seemed that they all looked at him in that next moment.

"I'm fine," she whispered as he examined her minor injury as if it was grievous.

Urian pressed a kiss to her bleeding wrist, and when he pulled away, a swatch of shadows layered over the minor injury there.

"Mine," he said again.

This time, though, it felt like a public declaration. A claim that needed an answer. And he looked at Katherine, feeling suddenly unsure. Whatever this was— this pressure, this uncertainty—he was at a loss to quelch it.

He found himself kneeling like a knight before a lord or lady.

"Urian?" she said shakily.

"My word, Katherine of Miller, that I'll do whatever it takes to keep you safe," he promised.

"That was just a scratch." She looked around, no longer the confident young woman he'd spent the day with, and Urian felt panic rise in his heart.

"All I ask is that you not leave me," he whispered. "I am *yours*."

She nodded, but her words were tense. "I'm not sure what's happening here."

"Neither am I," he confessed. The peril of being one of the rarest sorts of faeries was that there was no one to ask, no older *gancanagh* to answer questions.

A solitary faery Urian had never met stepped forward then. "Look away, you gawkers. Give the boy a little space to begin the bond with his lady."

She looked older, angry and nearly human. Aside from the skirt of dead rodents that draped across her hips, she might pass for any court's fey. The dead things were still dripping blood, though, and for that, Urian had no words.

Most of the assembled creatures scurried to obey her. When they did, she reached out and smacked Urian on the back of the head. "What are you doing, Urian? Give the girl a moment to think."

"Hey!" Katherine stepped forward, as if she was a force to reckon with instead of a woman barely through the awakening of the fey side of her heritage.

"I like *you*," the faery said. "Considerate thing, aren't you? Balance his impetuous self."

Then the creature grinned, flashing sharp teeth that looked more daggers than teeth. "You don't recognize me?"

Urian stared at her, let his vision slide to the corners of his eyes. Mortals thought that they were the only ones who used that trick, but some of the rawest magic could only be seen sideways.

"*Creature?*" he asked.

"Callisto," she said, curtseying.

Urian gaped at her as she stood, rolling her shoulders like she was stiff.

"Been a minute since I had no paws, hooves, or wheels." Callisto tilted her head, cracking her neck. "Been no need, though, has there? Mind your silly ass. Keep an eye on you, Sorcha says. Protect the pup."

"Pup?" Katherine echoed. "And you're the *car*?"

"Sometimes." Callisto looked at them both. "You can't marry the girl, Uri. You just met her."

"Marry?"

Callisto laughed, which to Urian's ears sounded like a war cry. Whatever she was, Callisto wasn't one to dismiss. He wasn't sure what she *was*, though. He'd rarely felt as young or inept as he did in that moment.

"You were offering a binding vow," Callisto said. "And if

this one"—she hooked a thumb toward Katherine—"is as impulsive as you . . ."

No one spoke.

Then Callisto clapped her hands together. "Boom. Wife. Husband. That's what you were doing, Uri."

He looked at Katherine. "I didn't mean to . . . I didn't know . . ."

"Lust faeries," Callisto muttered. "Can't leave them to their own. End up spending centuries pouting like your Da did. If not for Thelma in his path, we'd all have been dealing with the fall out of Irial and the scarred boy's terrible romance."

"The who?" Katherine asked.

"Last Dark King? This pup's da? Irial used to be all moon-eyed over a gancanagh who rejected him," Callisto explained.

"The gancanagh who is now the current Dark King," Urian added. "My father stole my mother's throne, her life, and then tossed his throne at his ex-lover rather than to his children where it ought to rightfully have gone."

Callisto wacked the back of Urian's head again. "Didn't remember you existed, did he?"

She sighed.

And Urian looked at her. "I think I like you better as a car . . . or a horse."

Callisto flashed sharp teeth at him in what he was fairly sure was a smile, not that he'd bet his life on it.

Then she sauntered off into the crowd with a repeated, "No weddings, pup!"

And Urian was left feeling far less confident than he was accustomed to feeling. He looked at Katherine, hoping she wasn't looking at him with tainted eyes. No faery in this world was omnipotent, so being smacked around by wild magic wasn't emasculating.

What he worried was that the revelation that Katherine had almost married him accidentally would send her fleeing.

She met his gaze, and instead of censure, he found joy. "Huh. Guess you like me as much as you said."

Urian's unexpected laugh escaped. "Told you."

"True." Katherine nestled close to his side. "Maybe we ought to start with dating instead of . . . you know . . .weddings."

"If you prefer," he agreed.

"I do," she said, then realizing what words she had just said, added quickly. "I do *prefer* dating."

"How about we grab a drink and talk?" he suggested, gesturing to a table laden with assorted wines and liquors. "Pick your drink, Katherine. I'll keep answering questions, the sort where we stay clothed."

Her answering smile was wicked in all the right ways. "For now," she murmured.

And somewhere in the throng of dancing faeries, Urian heard Callisto laugh.

Chapter Twenty-One

KATHERINE

They made their way to a table that looked like it still had roots on one end, as if a tree had simply bowed deep and the assembled faeries decided to rest their drinks on it before it straightened again.

"Why do I feel like this is a test?" she asked quietly.

Various faeries watched her, some subtly and others overtly. Unlike most of her encounters with the fey, these faeries didn't hide their notice of her. If anything, they seemed more interested than she could understand.

"No test, love, unless you want to take one." Urian gestured at the bottles. "What's your preference?"

Normal liquor was there, but there were a few that were very obviously something else. She realized that they were fey in some way or other.

One of the bottles looked like sunlight captured in a thick green glass bottle. Another looked like it was slick black ink writhing all on its own. A third bottle was more jug than liquor bottle. It seemed like ice was barely contained inside that one. A thin layer of rime seemed to crackle the bottle, and the table under it had a sheen as if it alone was frozen. Another looked empty, although she knew somehow that it wasn't. Something ethereal filled it. Yet another was filled with what looked like a bunch of thunderclouds or shadows.

Assorted other bottles, all less unusual, lined the table. It was those five that drew her attention, though.

"One of those five," she finally said.

Somehow, she knew that was the question. They were a test if she *wanted* to take it, he'd said.

"Which one?" he prompted. "If you want one . . ."

Katherine knew in her heart that there was only one she wanted, but she was afraid of making a mistake. "What happens if I pick the wrong one?"

"No one does if they trust their instincts." Urian kissed her cheek, and while he was close, he whispered, "You can avoid those drinks if you want, love. No pressure on *anything*, remember? No one will look upon you differently, and"—he pulled back and looked around—"if anyone did judge you, they'd have to answer to me."

Katherine looked at him, truly looked, and her heart felt like it was stuttering at the impossible adoration in his expression.

Faeries can't lie. She wondered if that meant that his affection was as real as it seemed. *Could he be confusing lust for love?*

That question felt too hard to process. She pointed at the table. "How?"

"Close your eyes," he said. "No different than my surly car. See with the part of you that's not mortal."

Katherine closed her eyes and counted, *one-two-three-four-five.*

On six, she opened her eyes and reached for the bottle

that was beckoning her. She tilted the ink-slick wine and poured it into a glass that Urian held out.

"Dark Court," he said simply.

"Which means what?"

The wicked look he gave her made her consider leaving the very public gathering of faeries. Instead, she lifted the glass to her lips and took a drink. It felt like swallowing shadows, and every bit of restraint she had shuddered as she took a second sip.

Urian took the glass from her hand before she could have a third sip, but rather than putting the drink on the table, he drank the rest and said, "*Gancanaghs* are often Dark Court. There are rare exceptions, of course . . . but you are of the Dark, Katherine of Miller."

Any illusion that the assembled group wasn't watching faded as Urian lifted a second bottle. Sunlight seemed to flash into the clearing as he opened it, and the wine he poured into the oil-slick remnants in the glass was thick like honey.

The crowd held a collective breath as he lifted the bright honey-wine to his lips and drained it, too. As he did, his eyes shifted so that it looked like light and shadow were twisting in his irises. A dark night with rays of light, a storm with flashes of lightning, Urian was not of one but *two* courts.

"To the exiled prince!" one of the faeries cheered.

As others took up the words, Urian chased the sunlight from his lips with another—albeit smaller measure--of that inky drink. There was more than liquor in these drinks, and she briefly wondered if the others would be as painful as the Dark Court drink was pleasurable.

She reached up to kiss him, but he stopped her with a raised hand.

He whispered, "First, I want to drown the light, Katherine."

"Why?"

For a moment, she saw him weigh his words, but he drank a long swallow of that inky liquor first.

When he pulled her in, she realized that he was hiding something, even though his smile was the look of the thoroughly intoxicated. A few sips ought not be reason for such a drunken smile.

But whatever liquor or secrets hid in those glasses, they weren't reason enough to refuse the kiss he pressed on her. Her lips parted, and Urian kissed her breath away.

She clutched him to her, as if he'd vanish in a blink.

When his hand slid down to cup her ass, all she could think of was a few hours earlier when he'd held her steady and led her toward bliss. A moan escaped her.

He tasted of shadows, like the wine but with something feral in between the dark and night that she'd tasted in her two sips of the wine from the Dark Court.

When he finally pulled back, Urian shifted away from the question she'd asked by saying, "No sunlight for you, Katherine. Not now. Not ever. Only shadows. That's what we'll do. Take *that* court, make it our own. Leave the sunlight to others."

And she was certain she was misunderstanding. *Take a court? Weren't all the thrones occupied?*

Urian spun her into a dance that seemed to be somewhere between a waltz and a tango, flirtation and promise, and Katherine decided not to ask questions tonight.

She had already learned more about her heritage—and court affinity—in one brief day than in most of her life. The rest of the questions could wait.

. . .

By the time Urian led her to a mossy patch of ground, Katherine had been greeted by at least twenty strangers. They were, like her, mostly halflings. They seemed more eager to meet her than the faeries that hung around the edges; at least that was her impression.

"Do they not like people who are mixed?" she asked quietly.

"Mixed?"

"Half-mortal," she clarified as he pulled her into his arms.

Urian settled her more solidly in his lap. He burrowed his nose against her throat, taking deep breaths like he needed to inhale her skin, like he had some hunger he had to fill in a way that was more than touch. "Darkness, Katherine. That's why some of them held back. You are cut from shadows. Not everyone likes that. Plus, you are mine—"

"No wedding, as far as I recall," she murmured, feeling more intoxicated now that they weren't dancing.

"Still mine." Urian nipped her throat. "I don't need a ceremony to know that you're my Dark Queen. Do *you*?"

"I don't know about queens, but I like this whole 'being yours' thing," she admitted. "A part of me feels like it's woken, and all I want is to be in your arms."

"All?" he prompted. "No dreams of ruling? Power? Wandering?"

"Honestly? Just you." She felt like she ought to be embarrassed by her admission, but she wasn't. Everyone probably dreamed of happily-ever-afters, but she'd been sure there was no such option for her. Hide from the fey, and never touch mortals. That had been her plan for a future.

Until Urian.

He looked at her like he was weighing thoughts he wasn't sharing, and a voice—one that sounded a *lot* like her mother—pressed her to ask questions.

Then Urian lowered his mouth to her throat.

For several moments, she let go of all her questions. She wasn't interested in politics or intrigue. "I might want to travel . . . kiss you in Paris, in Prague, and all the places out there."

He laughed, breath tickling her throat. "All the cities in the alphabet?"

"Yes, please."

He straightened and looked into her eyes. "Would that really be enough?"

"You?" She almost laughed until she realized that the seemingly arrogant faery was actually sounding insecure. "Seriously? *Yes,* Urian. Just you is more than enough. You are . . . I want this. You. This morning all I'd hoped for was answers to who I am and perhaps a few kisses . . ."

"Now?"

"Flirtation aside? I'm *happier* than I could've imagined when I walked toward you this morning."

He started to reply when she realized what she said. *Morning? Shit.* She looked around as clarity hit her.

"What time is it?" Katherine scrambled out of his embrace. "What time? Shit. Shit. Shit."

Urian looked up at the sky. "Two? Three? Somewhere between them. Dawn is still several hours away, Katherine."

He reached for her, tilting to the side to try to catch her and pull her back, and she realized that he was drunker than she'd thought.

As she swayed on her feet, standing unsteadily, she realized that *she* was feeling drunker, too. A few sips ought not equate to drunkenness.

"I need to go home," she insisted, tugging him as if she could force him to stand.

"My car is dancing around a bonfire." Urian gestured toward the car-turned-woman who was shrieking and leaping like something far more feral than anything there. "Go get her, though. We can try to . . ." He raised his voice, "Callisto!"

Callisto looked their way and laughed.

"Or not," Urian added quietly.

Katherine pulled her phone out of her pocket and turned it on, not really expecting signal, but it lit with one bar.

She texted her mother and her aunt both: AT A PARTY. ALL OKAY. NOT ABLE TO DRIVE. NO WORRIES, I AM SAFE FROM GOBLIN MEN.

"Goblin men?" Urian read over her shoulder. Between kisses, he said, "Goblins aren't real, you know?"

"Code," Katherine clarified. "So they know I'm really *me* when I text."

"Smart." Urian watched her mouth. "Beautiful and smart."

"You realize that you're drunk?" Katherine said, accepting his hand coming closer and lowering herself so she was straddling him, kneeling as she had done earlier when they were far more naked.

"Drunk on you," Urian whispered.

"And some weird wine," Katherine added with a laugh. "What is it?"

"Essence of the three original courts," Urian said. "Can only drink the one that would be a fit for you. The others will make you puke. Won't kill you or anything, just make you feel like you want to die. Like a hangover but worse."

"And you let me drink th—"

"*Let* you?" Urian pulled away to stare into her eyes. "I do not control you, Katherine. Not ever. I will play at it when we are naked if it brings you joy. And I'll give you control over me if *that* does, but aside from intimacy, no person ought to control another."

Katherine nodded. Hearing him say that even now made her want to stay exactly where they were. Drunk or sober, he was making perfect sense.

"Okay," she said. "I chose that."

"That's the problem with what we are, though, isn't it?" he whispered. "We steal control from any but another of our kind. A mortal is defenseless. A faery can still be drunk on us . . . *Gananaghs* are poison, Katherine. Even me."

"To everyone but me," she clarified. Her hands cradled his face, making sure he was looking at her. Her thought about his insecurity was right. For some reason, he had a dose of self-hatred in him that seemed at odds with reality.

"You choose to be with me?" he whispered.

"I am not swearing to eternity, Urian, but I'm right here. There is nowhere in the world I'd rather be."

"Even knowing what I am? Even knowing that I plan to kill my father?" Urian asked.

"Plan to *what*?"

"Kill Irial." Urian nodded drunkenly. "Pro'lly the Dark King, too. Dumbass that he is, he seems attached to Irial so . . ." Urian shrugged. "Remove them. Take the court. Make you my queen and—"

"Let's hold off on murder plots, okay?" Katherine smiled, hoping these were drunken ramblings. *Faeries can't lie.* She stared at him, and a part of her wasn't horrified that he spoke so casually about murder.

A more rational streak said that she wasn't going to go along with it. She had no interest in thrones.

"Make you my queen," he murmured, between kissing her collar bones again.

"Hard pass," she said.

"What?"

She turned and made sure she was holding his gaze. "I have a *lot* of other things I'd rather you concentrate on. Seriously, though, do you really need a throne? I don't."

He blinked at her, and she noticed that she was also slurring now. Over the last few minutes, she realized that she was now almost as drunk as he was.

"Why am I feeling drunker without drinking more?" she asked.

"Takes a few minutes to hit." Urian shrugged. "That's why I finished yours: to keep you from passing out."

"But you *also* had more," she half-objected, half-asked.

"Didn't want to kiss you with sunlight on my tongue and make you sick." Urian spoke the words like they were perfectly logical. "And I didn't want to drink sunlight first and have you think I was more bright rather than shadow. And Katherine?" He paused and leaned forward. "I cannot stop kissing you."

Katherine brushed her lips against his. "You're absurd."

"Nope. It would be absurd not to kiss you, so I did what I needed to do." Urian brushed his lips over her again. "When I'm king—"

"I bet kings are busy. All the time. People to command. Bills to pay." She mock-shuddered. "Sounds boring to me."

"You truly don't want a throne?" He pulled back and stared at her. "Even a little?"

Katherine shook her head. "Nope. I just want *you*. Travel. There's a whole world out there. Why would we want to stay here? Why would I want to share you with a whole *court*?"

Urian stared at her unblinkingly for a moment.

"Think of all the hours we wouldn't be kissing . . ." She had started this train of thought to explain that he was enough for her, but as she continued, she started to think about it practically. "I might be monstrous for saying this, but I don't want to share you *at all*. I mean, I'm not planning on locking you in a tower, but it's not the worst idea I've ever had."

He chuckled. "And what would you do with me if you had me locked away?"

"Shall I demonstrate?" She pushed him backward, and a flash of shadows raised up around them, like an inky veil covered in shimmering lights. *Sunlight,* she realized. Shadows and light.

"Privacy," he muttered. "I might not seem it, but I was born in a time when you don't let people look at your lady."

This time it was her that laughed. "My wicked, wicked gentleman. I thought you mentioned voyeurism earlier . . . Who knew you had a jealous streak?"

"Just with you."

And that, she thought, was wonderful.

She felt a little more okay with her selfishness knowing that he felt possessive over her, too. Surely that meant that he could leave off this desire for a throne, and then everything would be fine.

Chapter Twenty-Two

AISLINN

Aislinn felt restless. It wasn't unheard of to feel that way. She was the embodiment of Summer, impulsive where Winter was calm. At least that's what she used to think. Having fought alongside the current Winter Queen, Aislinn was no longer entirely sure that Winter was any calmer than Summer.

Maybe it was a question of what provoked sunlight and what provoked shadow more than anything.

"Where's your paramour?" Tavish asked as he walked into the aviary where Aislinn had been thinking.

"His place."

"And you are here because?" Tavish prompted. Had anyone else been so impertinent, she might have reprimanded them, but he was her advisor, her friend, her brother by choice.

"Thinking."

"About?" He stood at attention, despite their friendship.

The Summer Queen nodded at a bench she'd braided out of vines earlier while she was pondering.

Tavish sat, although his relaxed posture was still stiff.

"Would it be possible to hand my court over to Urian?" Aislinn asked. "Could I be a mortal? Or solitary? I mean, Keenan handed it over. Could I? Could Niall?"

"Theoretically?"

She nodded.

"Yes," Tavish said simply. "Why, though?"

"If it's that or another war . . ." Aislinn looked at him. "I don't want that again. I don't think proposing it to Niall would be wise, but if I just . . . I don't know . . . let go. Would it be so bad?"

"Go see your love," Tavish suggested. "Summer is meant for rejoicing, Ash. And I can't offer you anything to turn this mood away. A person who would sacrifice for their court, that's the definition of a ruler. You are asking yourself hard questions to keep us safe. That tells me that *you* are the queen we need."

She nodded.

"But right now, what *you* need we cannot give you." Tavish stood and held out a hand. "Go to Seth."

Aislinn left the loft and walked through Huntsdale toward the trainyard. Seth spent most nights in the loft, but sometimes his logical side needed the calm of his own home—and Aislinn was grateful for it, especially on days like this.

For a moment, when she walked toward the train that had once been her haven, that was *still* her haven if she were honest, she paused to marvel at the odd home he'd fashioned. He'd bought a few train cars years ago, and through a mix of ingenuity and engineering had converted them into a trailer-house.

The outside of Seth's train was decorated in murals. Beside the train was a garden where metalwork sculptures and flowering plants seemingly sprouted. For a moment, Aislinn looked at the plants. They thrived now that winter and summer were balanced.

The world thrives because of it.

"Seth?" she called as she stepped inside, avoiding a pile of books on the floor, grateful that she was immune to the limits of steel because she was a regent.

"Back here," Seth called from the second train car, which was where the tiny bathroom and his bedroom were.

She followed his voice to the second car and found him sitting on his bed with books, a notebook, and assorted pens.

"What's up?" He patted the mattress, inviting her closer. "Did we have plans?"

"No." Aislinn felt like a part of who she used to be was held in his possession, and as she sat next to him, she felt like the responsibility of being the Summer Queen slipped away. "I just needed you."

Seth nodded. "I'm right here, Ash. For as long as we are both able, I am yours."

Something there pricked her anxiety, as if there were a time or reason he would not be hers. The thought of that made her stomach twist. She had no desire to surrender *anything* that was hers—including Seth. She did, though, and often. They were always apart because he was off doing this or that, and she had to stay where she was.

"What if I wanted to hand over the court?" She said the words in a rush, looking at him. "To Urian. Maybe if I did that, he wouldn't hurt anyone in my court."

"Is that what you want?"

"Him not to hurt anyone? *Yes.*" Aislinn was certain of that much at least.

"To give up the court," Seth clarified.

And there was no way to answer that. The words she wanted to say would be lies, so she couldn't speak them. That was answer enough for Seth.

"So what's the real issue?" He pushed his books to the side, and in the next moment, he pulled her into his embrace. "Talk to me."

"The Wild Hunt wants to join my court." Aislinn plucked at his shirt absently, hating the barrier.

Seth grinned. Then he removed the shirt and pulled her close again. He dropped a kiss on the top of her head and teased, "Pushy."

"Needy," she corrected.

Silly as it might be, Aislinn was more relaxed just by touching his bare chest. She sighed and nestled into his arms. Later she'd be all the things she had to be—capable, strong, decisive, *vicious*—but right now, she was a woman in her lover's arms. That was what she needed: the sliver of normal life that he could still give her.

"Chela's offer felt like an insult to you," Seth surmised. "Judgment for how far you are willing to go for the Summer Court."

"Yes."

Seth kissed the top of her head again, keeping her tucked into his embrace, as if he knew that all the little touches soothed some anxiety that she couldn't quite voice.

"You want to protect them," Seth said. "The Summer Court has had centuries of abuse, suffering, loss. And you are their head. Their heart. It's only natural that you are protective—"

"Vicious." Aislinn glanced up at him. "Tavish says that's why. He thinks that's what Chela's offer says about me."

"He's not wrong." Seth stroked her hair gently, as he had when they'd first started to get closer. It seemed like a small thing after all they'd done since, but the small gestures of affection were as important as the joys she'd known in his arms.

"If I could purr, I would," Aislinn mumbled.

"What aren't you saying?" Seth prompted with a little hug. "You aren't just fixating on one word, one detail."

She filled him in on the conversation with Keenan. That *was* bothering her, too.

Seth snorted. "Sunshine is always melodramatic."

A laugh escaped her at that. Five years later, Seth was no more tolerant of the man who had tried to steal her affection. It shouldn't make her laugh, but it did. He trusted her, but he also held a grudge that made him possessive. Years later, he looked at Keenan with only thinly veiled irritation.

"Did you realize that he was asking Niall to watch over you back then because Niall was . . . addictive?" Aislinn hadn't really thought much about it at the time. She'd barely been making sense of her own changes at the time.

"Not at first. No idea why him, but when I started thinking things that weren't my sort of taste, I knew something was weird." Seth shrugged. "We're cool, though. Friends, and since I'm not mortal anymore, it worked out. Don't really like what Sunshine was willing to do to get rid of me, though. That sort of addiction kills people, you know?"

"My great-grandfather. . . he addicted Thelma. That's what it had to be, right?"

"Irial wasn't like that because he was a king at the time," Seth reminded her. "He wasn't addictive to your great-gran.

Your uncle is simply batshit to ignore that detail. He *has* to know that his mother didn't die because Iri loved her. Logically—"

"Not everyone is logical," Aislinn pointed out.

When Seth was silent, she caught his gaze. There was no doubt that he was hiding something. *Logical.* That was a hint. He said that word because he couldn't outright say it.

"Sorcha is involved," Aislinn muttered. "I fucking hate politics."

"Pretty good at them, though." Seth grinned. "You sussed that out with a single clue."

The Summer Queen rolled her eyes.

"You're the rightful Queen of Summer, Ash." Seth brushed her hair away from her face, letting the strands fall like silk through his fingers. "You're willing to do whatever it takes to protect them, even walk away."

"Keenan did the same."

Seth snorted. "Yeah, and at the final battle with that feathered menace, what did he do?"

Aislinn sighed. "Protected Donia."

"Abandoned everyone," Seth said.

"Same thing, though, wasn't it?" Aislinn glared at her love. "Would you let the world burn for me?"

"I'm not a king," Seth evaded, stabbing her heart with his words. "And you know better than to ask me that. If Sorcha thought I might die over here, she'd wall me up like a pet."

The thought of the High Queen's fondness for Seth, her adopted son, was enough to make Aislinn gnash her teeth. She was the one regent that they all had to fear. The oldest faery, the least sane now that her twin was dead, and she'd picked Seth to mother. Of all the mortal to pick, she'd bonded with Seth. The upside was that he was half-immortal now, but the downside was that no one could surmise what half of eternal meant—or what risks her love posed for all of them.

"I wanted this," Seth reminded her. "Chose a curse to be with you."

"And the High Queen would crush me like I was a sliver of glass if I spoke against her weird bond with you," Aislinn added. "I know the rules."

"So . . .?"

Aislinn sighed. "I appreciate the clue you carried back from Faerie. I appreciate that she lets you come home to me. I just sort of hate the whole mess sometimes."

Seth smothered a smile. "Says the temperamental Summer Queen with the Dark King's heritage in the mix . . ."

"Oh hush!" Aislinn poked him in the side. "I'm serious, Seth. Maybe I'm not cut out for being a queen."

He propped himself up on one arm and stared down at her. "Or maybe it's still new, and you have a bit of post-traumatic stress because there was a faery war, and you're in your twenties dealing with these things when every other regent is, I don't know, a hundred or thousand years old."

"Fair," she admitted in a quiet voice. "I still don't like it."

"I know." He kissed her forehead. "But you are amazing. As a queen. As a woman. You are everything good and bright, Ash."

"And this is why my advisor sometimes shrugs and says 'go see Seth.'" She smiled. "You make the impossible seem possible, Seth."

He stroked her arms and said nothing.

So she took a deep breath and admitted, "I hate how

often you leave me. I hate everything about that. I don't want to feel like I'm your last priority . . ."

Seth toyed with the piercing in his lip, staring at her, weighing words he wasn't saying. When he replied, it was only to say, "I love you, Ash."

And then, as with every other conflict they had, he kissed away her worries. His hands and mouth knew her body the way only an artist could. With practiced ease, he parted her thighs and set about reminding her of everything he knew about her needs and wants.

Seth knew her body, and he soon had her arching and begging. Soon, flowers burst into bloom as she went spiraling into bliss.

Before she could try to broach the subject, Seth pulled her over him and gave her control. Hands tight on her hips, he gave her everything in that moment—control, love, and adoration.

She told herself it was enough. She loved him. He loved her. It *had* to be enough. But a little voice kept pointing out that what he didn't give her was a promise of the future she craved more and more.

Chapter Twenty-Three

KATHERINE

Waking up on top of Urian was not on the list of things Katherine expected that morning. Waking up with any man *ever* was not on the list. *Gancanaghs don't get to do that,* her mother's voice whispered in her mind. But here Katherine was, tangled up in Urian.

He opened his eyes to look at her. "Are we good?"

And it seemed so human, so normal, that she smiled at him. "I mean, I thought I was pretty good, but I'm still interested in practice. And you"—she kissed him in the center of his chest—"are like world-class good, possibly award winning. Are there orgasm Olympics? Because if there are—"

Her words were cut off with a yelp as he covered her mouth with his. His arms came around her, cushioning her he rolled her onto her back on the mossy ground.

Katherine was fairly sure he was melting her bones. Hangover be damned! If this wasn't a cure for whatever ailed a person, it ought to be.

She was dazed when she looked up to see that he'd stood up and was holding his hands down to pull her to her feet.

"Would you want to go to Europe?" he asked.

"Well, sure but—"

"When? Tonight? Tomorrow?" He took her hands and tugged. "I think we should start in Scotland."

"With what money?" She laughed at the thought of just taking off like that. No plan. No anything. He seemed to have taken her drunken desire to travel to heart.

Urian looked at her and said, "I have more money than I can spend in our very long lifetime, Katherine."

She paused. "Are you serious?"

"You said you wanted to be with me, that travel was better than toppling kingdoms, so"—he knelt, keeping her hands in his—"want to run away with me?"

"Not marriage," she said quickly.

"Yet." Urian stared up at her. "The fey don't lie, Katherine. I cannot lie."

"Faeries misdirect and—"

"I want you in my life, at my side, in my bed, for as long as we exist in this lifetime." Urian paused, smiling at her, not commenting that she was trembling. "I know. I feel it in here."

He pulled her hand to his chest.

"My lungs. My heart."

And as much as the mortal part of her, the practical side, the faeries-are-deadly side said "wait!," Katherine wasn't *merely* mortal. She'd been changing since she met Urian. She was happy, excited, and it felt like the entire world was rolled out in front of her.

Experience, romance, travel.

He was offering her all her dreams. She could have everything.

Because of him.

"Faeries don't lie," she echoed.

"So?"

Katherine tugged, and he stood.

"Yes," she whispered.

"Yes?"

"*Yes*," she repeated, louder now. "I need to go home and pack."

"Do you? We can buy everyth—"

"I need to go home and tell my mother and my aunt," she added. "Then, I can go."

Urian stared at her, looking unsure.

"I'm too fey now to lie to you, Urian," she swore. "*Tonight*. We can leave tonight."

Urian picked her up, arms sliding around her waist, and kissed her breathless. Again. This was it, her forever.

Katherine's legs wrapped around him, and she tried to let all of her excitement and joy shine through in the way she kissed him.

Mine, she thought, not daring to say the word aloud.

No accidental weddings here!

But she was certain of this, of him, of *them*.

"What about a hotel room tonight?" she suggested when he pulled back. "Go somewhere. I don't know . . . L.A.? New York? Somewhere with an international airport, and then we can decide where to fly to."

"Perfect." He let her slide down so her feet were back on the ground. For a moment, he paused, and she knew he had questions.

"What?"

"Do you want me to meet your mum?" Urian looked both awkward and willing at once. "I'm not sure if that will make her feel better or worse. Me being what I am and—"

"What *we* are," Katherine corrected. "She can't be upset with what you are unless she hates what I am."

He gave Katherine a look.

"Fine. It will probably be easier talking to her on my own, but . . . just like two hours?" She squeezed his hand, and they headed toward the car.

Luckily, Callisto was back in car shape, and Katherine tried not to wonder what happened to the dress of bloodied rodents that the car wore when she was in human-ish shape.

"We are grateful for the ride," she said quietly as she slipped into the passenger seat.

The car radio was silent. Maybe Callisto was a little hung over, too.

Katherine wasn't asking any questions of Callisto. Truth be told, she felt a little uncomfortable thinking that the car was also a person. Instead of thinking too long on that, Katherine waited for Urian to climb into the driver's side of the car.

"Will Callisto come to Europe with us?" she asked him once he was settled.

"If she chooses," he said. "I never really know what to think with her. I certainly wasn't expecting her to show up and slap me a few times."

The engine turned on with a roar.

The radio switched on to play "I've Been Everywhere" by Johnny Cash. It wasn't clear whether it meant that Callisto was done with travel, or not, but Katherine suspected that they were going abroad without the car—which was a little bit preferable in her opinion. The car was fine when she was a creature, but in woman-shape Callisto was more than a little terrifying.

And a bit of a third wheel when Katherine was setting out on a romantic adventure with Urian.

All that was left was for Katherine to tell her mother, and then she could start her new adventure.

URIAN

When Callisto stopped a few blocks away from the building where Katherine resided, her doors opened, and a clip of a woman saying, "You can't stay here" came on the radio.

"You never used to talk this much," Urian said.

The car engine revved, and before the doors were even closed, Callisto drove away, spitting gravel and dust.

"I don't think I can apologize for her," Urian told Katherine, wiping dirt from her face. "She never communicated until she met *you*."

"Aww, poor Urian. Do you think she just likes me better?" Katherine patted his cheek, wearing a faux sympathetic look.

"I do." Urian shook his head. "Makes sense, though. You're definitely prettier, and I bet you're a lot nicer."

Katherine's laughter was the reward he sought, so he preened a bit at hearing it. If he could gather each giggle, each smile, each flutter of her eyelids like jewels, he would. It felt like there was a hole inside him he hadn't noticed until her. She made him feel complete, that secret feeling that he was not *enough* was eased. Obviously, she didn't change everything about him, but she changed enough that he was grateful in ways he wanted her to understand.

"A lifetime of your attention and love isn't going to be enough for me," he told her. "We'll find a castle, build a moat, fill it with monsters. No one will get near you. I'll keep you safe and—"

"Wrong century, pretty," she said dryly. "And I'm not interested in being your damsel."

"Fine. We'll find the castle, build a moat *together*, fill it with monsters we pick out *together*. No one will get near you *or* me. I'll keep you safe, and you keep me safe. Better?" He caught her hand in his as they walked through town. Just two *gancanaghs* in a desert town. "I wasn't born in the same century as you, Katherine, and I hadn't expected . . . *you*."

She glanced at him. "Well, a castle would give us space for all my fantasies . . ."

"Keep talking," he teased.

"Lock you away until I get tired of you."

"Would you?" he asked, feeling that insecurity that had only ever come since meeting her. He knew what he was, and no one—fey or mortal—looked at a *gancanagh* without a sizzle of lust. He was, in a word, irresistible.

Except to another gancanagh. She could destroy him. *Like Irial destroyed my mother. Like he reputedly destroyed the current Dark King.*

"Lock you away? Most definitely." Katherine squeezed his hand.

"No. Get tired of me."

Katherine paused and reached up to pull him down for a kiss. Her lips tasted like something he hadn't known could exist in the world. Her kiss was as if every flavor he could want was right there: every breath, every need. His free hand clutched at her, as if willpower alone could keep them from needing to exhale, as if need was enough reason to forego breathing.

When she pulled back, her words feathered over his lips. "I don't think I'll get tired of you anytime soon. Possibly ever. I haven't known you long enough to give you a vow, even though I feel like I could." She stared at him as if she could will him to understand. "We just met, Urian. And until you, I never even talked to a faery other than my father. You have to give me more than a minute here."

A coil of fear in his belly unraveled. He was used to being desired, but this raw gnawing need he felt for her was new. If he had his way, he'd follow her inside while she packed.

"I don't want to be apart," he whispered. "Ever."

"For a minute. My mom . . . I don't want her meeting you," Katherine confessed. "It's silly, but what if because my dad was what we are and *you* are, too, . . . what if it makes her sick to see you? What if—"

"It doesn't work that way."

"Are you positive?" Katherine looked more like a warrior than a girl who had been hiding from the fey. Eyes glittering. Chin up. Shoulders back. She was frightening.

"I'm fairly sure, but if you want me to wait out here, I will." Urian traced her face with his fingertips, as if she were a painting he couldn't believe was right there to behold.

Mine.

She caught his wrist, pressed a kiss to the palm of his hand, and said, "I want this back later."

Then she was gone, vanishing inside a dingy building not fit for the queen she was. She might not want him to topple courts for her, but he'd build her a veritable queendom of her own. Raze small countries. Borrow the crown jewels. Whatever it took, Urian would make sure she was happy.

And that way she'll never leave me.

Letting Katherine walk away, vanish into the building where he'd just been waiting for her for days, took more self-control that Urian was used to employing. It wasn't that he was accustomed to always getting his way, but he wasn't accustomed to caring terribly much if others had wants that weren't his.

A few moments passed and then he saw Katherine at the window of her room, the room she was leaving tonight to go with him, and he lifted one hand to her.

She laughed and made a *shoo*-ing gesture.

Then the curtain dropped, blocking her from his gaze.

A horrible fear rolled over him, tugging him under a wave of terror the likes of which he hadn't ever felt.

Run, the order reverberated through him. *Do I need to smack you again?*

"Callisto," he said. "Where are you?"

Can't explain. Now, run, Uri. Run like the hounds are chasing you.

"What do—"

Run. Or they'll find her, too.

Whatever else Urian knew, he was certain that Callisto was his friend, an ill-mannered, dead-thing wearing, blood-thirsty maniac, but still, she was his friend.

Running without aid of a car was ludicrous, but he didn't see another option just then. He felt as if the very ground had become the pulse of war drums. Threads of something wet seemed to be sliding along his spine, and if he wasn't trying to run as fast as two legs could carry him, he might reach back to see if there was really something dripping down his skin.

Urian ran faster than he thought his body could go, but he felt hot puffs of something fetid. He felt creatures' breaths brushing the backs of his legs.

Run.

He heard teeth gnashing close enough that he pushed himself even harder.

Safety was still possible. He saw Callisto in the distance, engine running, door open. He simply had to reach her.

Don't look back. Run!

The hooves thundered over the ground like earthquakes, rattling his bones, making him think that the force of it would somehow slip under his skin. The ground was being carved by heel and talon, and he could taste the dirt that the creatures were slicing from the earth.

Despite all the willpower he possessed, Urian still looked back.

All that was behind him was a panting, heaving morass of violence. He couldn't see much, but it was enough. He stumbled.

The copper tang of blood filled his nose. The dust coated him like a weight to slow him. His muscles screamed as they twisted and steered him away from Callisto, and he realized that there was no escape.

"Precious little hare," a woman crooned.

Not a woman. Hound, Callisto said. *I'm sorry. I had no idea they were sent for you.*

It was one of the longest statements she'd ever made to him.

"The Hunt," Urian said and the surge of monstrosity

knocked him to the ground. "My father not willing to come see me? Has to send you to do his bid—"

"Irial did not send me." The Hound looked down at him with laughter dancing in her eyes.

"Then who? His--"

"A pretty little ray of sunshine." The woman patted her steed. "Vicious thing, Summer is."

And Urian bowed his head.

"No begging?" The Hound's boot was on his neck somehow.

He'd fallen, collapsed perhaps. His whole body shook from a twist of fear and exhaustion. And a woman was standing over him, boot on his neck.

Urian said nothing. He was not going to beg. They could take him to the Summer Court, and he would apologize for the whole stabbing incident and—

The boot slammed into his face, and the rest of the thought was drowned in pain and blood.

Chapter Twenty-Five

AISLINN

The Summer Queen felt the roll of terror in a different way this time. An almost energizing flutter crept over her.

"The Hunt approaches," she announced.

Without another word, she walked out of the loft and into the park that was part of her court. As she waited, Aislinn looked at the area that she'd expanded. There had been a parking lot to the western side, a street that lined the eastern edge, and the next block over had been a series of shops that she had purchased. The park now stretched, plants growing through the ruined remains of the buildings. One apartment building, which the residents had all been paid handsomely to sell, was now a structure of stone and plant--suitable for the Hunt to call their home.

Nervously, Aislinn hoped that she'd not been presumptuous to do so, but if she had, well, there were plenty of things to do with the new block of the city that she'd acquired. This was her home, and unlike the last Summer regent, she wasn't interested in relocating constantly.

So she'd been slowly expanding.

This time, however, it was rather vast and obvious. Once Winter noticed, they would have an issue. A part of Aislinn thrilled at the thought. *Look what I did! Look at how strong the Summer has become!*

"We will not apologize to the Dark or to Winter for our expansions," Aislinn told Tavish.

He grinned. "Why would we? We have not stolen what was theirs."

The Hunt filled the far end of the park, the side where Aislinn had been expanding, and the Summer Queen decided that it was time for more of a statement than was her usual way.

Sunlight took shape, as if the beams of light were liquid gold, and around them, she wove flowers. Maybe it was silly, girlish even, but she liked to twist flowers into everything.

They were summery, right?

Deep red wild roses twined around the sunlight throne she'd built at a whim, and the Summer Queen took her seat to watch the Hunt surge into her territory. They were welcome, especially if they brought quarry, but it was an odd feeling that rolled over her—no longer simple fear.

"Is it different for you?" she asked Tavish, who was standing at her side when the next wave hit.

"Softer." He looked fascinated, and there was no doubt that he would be off to scrawl in one of his journals as soon as he was free to do so. Her advisor was an unrepentant researcher, and over the last five years, he'd apparently been chronicling the courts.

Not just hers, either.

Tavish had been working on a memoir of sorts, stories about the Summer King before Keenan, stories about Niall, stories about various encounters with the now-dead Winter

Queen Beira. It was more of a chronicle of the courts, a reference for Aislinn.

"Details for your novel," she teased him, as they watched the Hunt come at them.

"Ash . . . we've discussed this. I'm writing a history of—"

"Sure, but you *could* publish it as a novel, make yourself a nest egg." Aislinn watched a nerve twitch in his cheek. Honestly, she wasn't sure why it was such a terrible idea. No one believed in faeries these days. Not really. There were rare exceptions, people who gathered at festivals and listened to music played on medieval instruments, but by and large, the world relegated faeries to the same fiction as actual make-believe things like ghosts or vampires.

"The approach of the Hunt has shifted because of their changing fealty," Tavish remarked, stepping off the dais that she had built around and under them, lifting her advisor and her impromptu throne up higher.

She added grooves to the thing, creating a stepped pyramid with her at the top like a sun goddess.

Tavish strode forward, descending far enough that anyone approaching would have to cross him to touch her. He was her most loyal guard as much as one of her most trusted advisors. In truth, he was close to a brother to her—family by choice—so she knew he would step toward any danger that befell her.

This was curiosity, though. He wanted to understand the change in how he felt about the Hunt, how their change in fealty changed the way the court reacted to them. From the looks on a few of her court's residents, they were equally curious.

"I still feel the sense of foreboding," Aislinn told him. "But I don't want to run."

"Nor should you," Chela said as the first of the Hunt slid to a stop that kicked soil and flowers through the air, as if she could somehow hit Tavish with flowers as if they were weapons.

Chela grinned at him. "Tavish. Looking spry for an old man."

"Gabriela," he replied formally.

That *was* her title, but Aislinn felt like the shift between them meant that she had leave to call the huntress by her first name. She smiled and said, "Chela."

"Ash," Chela returned the informality with a quirk of a smile that made Aislinn want to step forward.

"I trust you are well," Aislinn said idly, not yet rising from her sunlit throne.

The rough woman grinned, feral teeth and sharp edges. There was blood on her cheek, but it looked like rouge on her. "And victorious."

"Good hunt?" Aislinn looked past her, toward the seething mass of muscles and shadow. They weren't moving now, but the whole of the Hunt shifted and writhed. Motion even when still, they were a fascinating force.

And Aislinn couldn't resist the impulse to wade into those shadows. They felt like they were connecting to her, not directly but through Chela, through their Gabriela. She stood, not vanishing her throne, and held a hand toward Chela.

Chela laughed, but she strode up the pyramid and took Aislinn's hand. "Afraid you'll fall without me there, too?"

"Not at all," Aislinn murmured, fairly sure that she wasn't missing the flirtatious layers of meaning in those words.

The Hound, holding Aislinn's hand aloft, escorted her to

the bottom of the pyramid and gestured to the Hunt. "Walk among us, Summer Queen. Behold our power."

As the two of them stepped forward, the crowd parted without a spoken word. The breath of dog-like creatures huffed hot on Aislinn's bare ankles and feet. Creatures snorted or chuffed, exhaling plumes of heat against her bare arms and neck. No Hound moved. Their boot-clad feet didn't shift or step out of place. They were steady statues as Chela and Aislinn walked forward.

At the heart of the crowd, she saw the quarry.

Hanging limp, held upright only by the hands clutching his arms, was Urian. His feet were bare and bloodied. Thorns and rocks were embedded in his exposed flesh. His jeans were torn, and the tops of boots were around his ankles like strange wide bracelets.

Aislinn glanced at Chela inquiringly.

"Prey runs, Ash." Chela smiled, a cruel twist of lips baring her teeth. "If he faltered, we'd have carried him. He didn't." She shrugged, but the look she gave Urian was impressed. "Even after he wore out the boots, he ran."

"He ran until he couldn't stand," Aislinn murmured.

She understood why Chela was impressed by Urian, but it changed nothing. He was the one who came into her court, stabbed her advisor, and threatened her. The Summer Queen had no room for mercy.

With a blink, she fashioned manacles of sunlight and thorns around Urian's wrists. To them, she attached chain of vine, thick gnarled wood that was stronger than steel, and in the heart of it, she twisted sunlight and sand. They would burn, abrade, and restrain her enemy—but it was not painful iron or steel. She wanted Urian to fear her, but she wasn't going to expose him to steel to achieve that goal.

Unless this doesn't work . . .

She handed the end of the chain to Chela.

Then Aislinn stepped forward, so that she was in front of her uncle.

When he didn't look up, she pulled a deluge from a nearby cloud, soaking him with cold water and tiny pebbles of hail.

"What the h—"

Aislinn grabbed his face, stopping words and forcing him to look at her. "I don't believe we finished our conversation, uncle."

He blinked at her, trying to speak.

Then Aislinn released her hold. "Until I am satisfied that you are no threat to me or mine, you will be a guest of my court."

"Fuck you," Urian said.

Aislinn raised both brows. "*Truly*? That's your response? I knew faeries matured slowly, but . . ."

When he said no more, Aislinn turned to Chela. "I've renovated a few things. Expanded my immediate domain." She kept her voice casual as if it was of no consequence to rebuild a section of the city. "Would you like a tour of the area I've made to show my welcome of the Hunt?"

Chela's smile did odd things to Aislinn's belly.

"Of course," Chela said. "Oh, Summer Queen?" She waited until Aislinn was looking directly at her. "There was another halfling with him. I could smell—"

"I'll kill you if you touch her," Urian said.

Aislinn smiled, knowing in that moment that she looked as vicious as Tavish had accused her of being. "When you are rested, would you collect her for me? Perhaps my uncle would be more willing to make the necessary vows if he had a bit of incentive . . ."

Urian struggled, throwing his entire body against the restraining force of the Hounds who had hold of his arms. "I'll rip your hearts out and feed them to you while you're dying. I'll--"

His words cut off as Chela surged forward and punched him hard enough that he was suddenly limp.

"Hold this," she said to one of the Hounds, and then she extended her hand toward Aislinn. "Show me our new digs, Ash. Then we'll figure out where to put that one and go fetch his paramour. Her scent is all over him. It shouldn't take long to retrieve her, but we could use a rest before we go."

Aislinn nodded and led the Hound toward the building that she'd renovated.

Chapter Twenty-Six

KATHERINE

When she walked into the apartment, Katherine saw her mother and aunt exchange looks, and her gut reaction was to apologize. They had rules, and she knew that. A text wasn't enough. She knew they *expected* her to apologize.

She didn't, though; the fact was that she wasn't a child. She'd followed their rules, hidden away from half of her heritage, and she'd had no idea that there were other options.

"Curfew was—"

"Absurd." Katherine interrupted her mother. "It's absurd to even have a curfew at my age. I'm not a kid. You might treat me like one, but I'm not. I'm in my *twenties*."

"Kitty Kat . . ." Octavia Miller looked like someone had just stalled her heart. "The fey age differently, so I just didn't know how mature you were. Do we use mortal numbers? Court those years? Or are you like them? A few decades is barely adult to a full fey. Better to be safe, right?"

Guilt flared, and Katherine tried to sound less confrontational as she continued, "I get it, but I'm not one or the other. I'm half, and I am *not* a child. I've lived you way for all these years, now . . . I'm going to go away for a while."

"Because . . .?" her mother prompted.

Katherine didn't look away. "I told you I met someone."

"Is he human? Or . . . *not?*" Aunt Ida looked around, peering into shadows as if she could see the unseen by sheer willpower. "Or is he here right now? Hidden from us but here?"

Katherine shook her head. "I wanted to talk to you without him. And I want to pack a few things before I go." She shrugged, trying to act like this wasn't hard. She didn't want to hurt her mom or aunt, but she also couldn't stay here. She was completely certain of that. In a gentle voice, she added, "I'll check in with you periodically, so you don't worry, but it's time for me to go. Past time, really."

Her mother looked like tears were glimmering in her eyes. "You're rushing it. You can take baby steps. Get a place. Jose said the apartment on the ground floor is about to come open. Ida and I were talking. You'd still be here, but your . . . friend could visit in your own place that way."

Katherine looked at them, and the words she wanted to say warred with her love for them. They were her family, her shelter, and she felt a fierce loyalty to them. She sat down with a flop. "I love you, you *get* that, right?"

They nodded.

Her mom started to say something else, but Katherine didn't want to fight. "I'm not *asking,* Mom. I'm telling you. I've changed. I feel it. I can't hold the steel on the shutters now. I am sure of it. It's like something in me that was a bonfire waiting for a spark. And I woke up."

Her mother stared at her with an awkward sort of understanding. "Your sort of faery is prone to—"

"Lust," Katherine finished.

"Yes, that. It doesn't mean you have to leave home for that," her mom said.

"It does. It means exactly that. I want to go with him. No one is coercing me, tricking me, or anything. I want to go." Katherine didn't know how to explain, but she felt an insistence inside that she wander. Maybe Urian woke it, but it was *her* impulse.

"So you're just going to become a homeless person? Because of a faery you just met?" Ida asked, sounding angrier than Katherine had ever heard her. "Why would you trust him? He could say anything. Your dad told us how monstrous they were, Katherine. Don't be ridiculous. Plenty of people make decisions with their"—she gestured below the waist—"but you're *smarter* than this. Sex isn't worth ruining your life."

"I am one of 'them,'" Katherine said. "These monstrous things? I'm as much them as human. I know you taught me to fear and hate them, but did you ever think what that said to me? Did it ever occur to you that you were asking me to hate myself?"

Her mother and aunt exchanged looks, but Katherine was done. She knew it wasn't going to go easily, even if she came alone. They were prejudiced in their way, hating her for the part of her that scared them. That's all prejudice really was: fear. It festered into hate, and too often into violence. But at the heart, it was fear.

They are afraid of faeries.

I am fey.

How can they think I don't need to go away?

Katherine walked to her room and started to pack. She wasn't taking much. Some clothes, toiletries, and a notebook were all she really needed. It struck her that a life moving from town to town had prepared her for this in a way she hadn't realized: travel light, take only the essentials. Her life was not weighed down by things.

"Take a few weapons," her mother said, coming to stand in the doorway. "If you're doing this, do it right."

She was holding out a short sword in a leather sheath. "This was your father's. Metals the fey can touch. I saved it for you." Then she walked over to the suitcase and put a dagger in it. "I had this one made. The hilt is safe for faeries to touch. The scabbard is, too."

"But the blade isn't?" Katherine guessed.

"Exactly. Sharp and steel." Her mother's smile had an almost vicious edge to it. "Anyone hurts you? You have this. A weapon you can wield, that is poisonous to them."

"You're terrifying sometimes," Katherine said.

"I'm a mother." Octavia opened her arms. "And I'd slaughter anyone who hurt you, Kitty Kat."

Katherine let herself be held close and tight. "You aren't mad at me?"

"I'm worried, but I understand. You are your father's daughter. So of *course*, you want to roam and meet people and fall in love . . . I knew this day would come, and maybe I'm mad at myself, too. I swore I'd be ready, but I'm not." She pulled back and stared at Katherine. "But don't forget me, okay? I want visits and calls."

"Definitely."

Her mother nodded, and they finished packing together. It wasn't as comfortable as they usually were together, but it wasn't the slamming of doors that it had seemed like it would be at first.

Just before she left, Katherine paused as Aunt Ida came into the room.

"I think this is terrible," she said. "But, you can come home when you realize that. The door is always open. I won't even say 'I told you so.'"

Katherine sighed. "And I won't remind you how wrong you are right now when I return. I'm sure of myself." She looked at her mother. "I have great examples, and I am certain of this. Urian is the one for me. I'm not marrying him this week or anything--"

"Katherine!"

"Look. When you know, when you're what I am, what Dad was, you just . . . know." Katherine realized what she was saying as she spoke. She *did* know. She was as sure as he was about her feelings. Hurriedly, she said her goodbyes.

She had to tell him.

Maybe a wedding wasn't a terrible idea. Not today. But maybe sooner than she realized initially.

When Katherine left the building, she had a suitcase and a satchel. It wasn't much, but it was all she needed—other than Urian. A wide smile stretched over her face at the thought of days and nights and months with him. Everything seemed to happen so quickly, but maybe that was the upside of the no-lying limits. She felt like she could trust easily because everything he said *had* to be truth. I mean, sure, he could misdirect or omit things, but he spoke directly and clearly. She knew he was as invested as she was.

But when she left the building, stepped outside into the New Mexico sunlight, he wasn't there.

"Uri?" she called several times, circling the building.

No one answered. There were no faeries anywhere she could see, and that was odd. Someone was always nearby.

"Is anyone here?" she called, louder now

Katherine felt like there was something wrong, but there weren't any clues that supported her feeling. He was a guy, and he left. That happened—especially since he was a *gancanagh*. Had she imagined his sincerity?

He wasn't lying, she thought. *I know it!*

She walked along the street, thinking that maybe he was at a store. Maybe he was tired of waiting on his makeshift throne. She looked into the coffee shop, the used bookstore, the gem and mineral store, a pawn shop. Nothing but strangers staring back at her.

The closest she came to a clue was Gina, Urian's friend. They'd talked, texted a bit, but she was still Urian's friend first.

"Hey," Katherine said, feeling like the dumbest sort of woman. "Have you seen Uri around?"

"Uri, huh?" Gina grinned. "Uh huh. So, I guess you weren't immune to falling for that charm after all?"

"Guess not." Katherine didn't feel even a flicker of shame. She felt lucky.

Gina motioned to the hilt sticking up over Katherine's shoulder. "Any reason you're walking around with a big assed sword on your back?"

"Helps with posture?" Katherine said lightly.

Gina laughed. "Uh huh. Expecting trouble?"

"Not really . . .? I don't know, but I have an overprotective mom," Katherine started. Her words died when Callisto strolled into the store. She was still wearing a skirt of dead things, bits of flesh and fur clinging to them in patches.

"Ummm. . . hi?" Gina said.

Callisto ignored her and stared at Katherine.

"He's gone," Callisto said. Her voice was gravel and rage, as if there was something she might break if only she could figure out what it was.

"We had plans," Katherine objected, feeling the fool for trusting any man. "He said we were going away. He—"

"It wasn't his choice, girl!" Callisto's hands were balled into fists. "They came for him."

"Who?" Gina asked.

"The Hunt." Callisto stared into the distance, but there was nothing out there but scrub and cactus as far as Katherine could see. "And if you stay here, Katherine, they'll come for you next."

Katherine shook her head. No one knew her; no one knew anything about her. Until Urian, she'd successfully avoided the world of faeries. One day and night with him, and everything was changing.

"They have your scent." Callisto seemed to be struggling with words. "On him. You marked scent all over him. You can't hide from them if they have your scent."

At first Katherine couldn't follow, but then Callisto made several crude gestures and said, "The sexing? You did that with him. He smells of you."

It was obvious that the words weren't quite right, but Katherine understood all the same—and so did Gina, who was giving her an appraising look. Katherine ignored that for now and said, "And so the Hunt knows my, err, *scent,* but why would they come after me?"

"To break Urian? To take you as the captive? You are a halfsie." Callisto scowled. "We must hide you."

"I thought you *just* said you couldn't hide from the

Hunt?" Katherine tried not to think about what it would mean to be taken by them or what Urian was suffering.

Katherine shot a look at Gina, who was clearly trying to follow the odd conversation. "Gina, I think I need to go with her."

"Do you need me to do anything?" Gina asked.

Katherine shook her head. "I think this one is on me. The Hunt . . . they're the things that *faeries* fear, so I don't think exposing you to them is a great idea. Just stay away from any strangers that show up in town, I guess. And keep a phone handy in case he calls you . . . ? Maybe he'll escape."

Callisto snorted.

"We go to Faerie." Callisto shifted into a great winged beast before the word was fully out.

Gina gaped at her. And Katherine was fairly sure she looked as stunned as Gina.

Callisto wasn't precisely a *dragon*, but more of a nightmare of what a dragon could be. Skeletal ribs were exposed, bits of furred flesh stretched over the bottom of the rib cage like a patchy rug. Her tail was a spiked thing flicking anxiously. The monster's face, though, was the thing that stole all of Katherine's words. Lizard eyes, lidless and black, stared at Katherine, and Callisto's mouth was that of a smiling serpent. Fangs the size of a human's leg jutted down over her lower jaw, and something pearl-white dripped from her teeth.

Venom.

Sure, riding a venomous monster to Faerie where halflings were kept prisoner sounded great. Her dad had mentioned that some faeries carved out the eyes of people with Faerie Sight, and some kept them and halflings pris-oner. Going to Faerie sounded like an awful idea. Of course, so did being a prisoner of the Wild Hunt.

"Stay safe," Gina said in a squeaky voice.

Katherine nodded and then looked at Callisto. "We need to rescue Urian. I'm not going there and hiding. Promise me you won't leave me there?"

The creature, Callisto's form currently, nodded. She licked the venom from her teeth and smiled.

"I'm not sure I make the best knight, but since Urian went all damsel in distress, this is where we are," Katherine muttered as she climbed Callisto's leg and onto her back.

Katherine's boots were good for gripping, but nothing about using anyone's exposed ribs as steps made her feel okay.

And then they were off. Katherine looked down and real-ized that her suitcase—and a steel bladed dagger in it—was held in Callisto's talons, like a fish in the grip of an eagle. Despite everything, the absurdity of that detail made Katherine laugh.

Better laugh than cry at the things that could go wrong.

Chapter Twenty-Seven

AISLINN

Aislinn kept herself several steps ahead of Chela inside the building that she'd been re-designing for the Hunt. Everything she knew—which was admittedly scant—said that they bedded down in groups often. Steeds and riders shared stable stalls, or a mix of the massive creatures and Hounds in veritable piles. Just in case, though, she'd also left the top five floors of the building as apartments. The idea of never having privacy seemed peculiar.

"Are you nervous?" Chela asked from somewhere behind her.

Aislinn paused and glanced back.

"You've not stopped talking." Chela gestured at the plant-filled stables. "These don't require that many words, you know. Walls, floor, soft bedding that you grew for us."

Aislinn tried to sound regal as she answered, "I want you to be happy. You do the court a great service by—"

"The court?"

"The Summer Court. *My* court." Aislinn did not flinch or

step back as Chela stepped up to her, too close, too close by far.

"I'm not here for the court," Chela said, leaning in to sniff right next to Aislinn's throat. The Hound made a sound that would be called a purr, except Hounds don't purr. "I picked you, Ash. Bloodthirsty, powerful queen. The court is a reflection of you, just like any court, but make no mistake, we are here because of you, because *I* chose *you*."

For a moment, Aislinn stared out at the flowering clematis, the blossoms so pink they might have been red in another moment. The delicate petals that were darker at the edges symbolized mischief and ambition, and Aislinn had set them to grow all over this building.

"Like pretty red lips," Chela said, following Aislinn's gaze, but not stepping out of her space. "Are you ambitious, Ash?"

Aislinn nodded, not at all surprised that Chela understood the language of flowers. The Hound was thoroughly unexpected.

"Wrapping around everything, claiming it like you did this building." Chela's words weren't a literal question, but they still sounded like one. They felt like something else though, especially as they brushed over Aislinn's skin and left shivers in their wake.

Aislinn nodded again.

"Why wouldn't I bring my Hunt to you? To your court?" Chela added.

"Is that why?" Aislinn forced herself to ask, looking up at Chela's eyes. "The *only* reason why?"

Chela's smile was wicked and beautiful. "Can you think of any other reason?"

"Maybe . . .?" Aislinn's pulse was somehow in her throat, making her voice sound rough.

"Just maybe?" Chela looked like all the trouble in the world just then.

And Aislinn was confused. There was no other word for it. She shouldn't be feeling this, reacting like this. She might be fey now, but she was mortal first, and as a mortal she'd fallen in love with an amazing man. He'd risked everything for her. Sure, she'd been tempted by Keenan—tempted enough that when Seth was away in Faerie the first time, Aislinn had considered the thought of forever with a king at her side, with Keenan at her side, but he hadn't loved her like he loved Donia.

And I didn't love him that way.

But in the five years she'd been queen, only Seth had been in her bed. She was happy. Why was she reacting to Chela this way?

Aislinn cleared her throat and said, "I'm sure the Dark Court misses you. I expect them to come here once they learn that you switched your loyalty to Summer."

Chela laughed. "Let them. I answer to no man. No Hound does. We are our own masters, and we make our beds where we choose, for however long we choose."

"Gabriel—"

"Fathered children with countless mortals," Chela said. "He had needs that are not my own."

"I thought you two were mated?" Aislinn rarely felt her mortal roots as clearly as she did when trying to understand centuries-long relationships. In her life, short as it had been, she'd loved one man. She'd never really dated before Seth.

Other than sort of dating Keenan.

Seth was gone only a few months, and I was ready to . . .

Chela seemed to take pity on Aislinn's awkwardness. She said, "I loved Gabe for over six hundred years. He was my mate, my leader in the Hunt, and if I had any desire to have pups, I'd have had his. I would have bathed in the blood of any who harmed him." She smiled in that way of people remembering things they were not sharing. "He liked to think I'd object if I discovered his mortals, if I knew he'd had yet another pup. So—" she shrugged "—I kicked his ass from time to time and reminded him where he was to bed down each night."

"But you didn't really mind?" Aislinn surmised.

"Monogamy is a mortal concept, Ash. It works for Donia and Keenan because they were so wrapped up in mortal matters. Maybe it will work for you and Seth because you *were* mortals." Chela shook her head. "Hounds? Not really built for it. I like the look of you, the scent of you, the way your eyes dilate when you see me looking."

"So you came to my court because . . . ?"

"Because you smell like trouble and hunger," Chela answered. "If that means you'll send us out to hunt, great. If it means that you'll expand your territory and start a fight with other courts, great. If it means you realize you ought to learn to fight better, I'm here for that, too."

Aislinn nodded, thinking that was the end of the answer, but then Chela put a hand out to stop Aislinn. Chela's hand was outward, palm flat, but not quite touching Aislinn's stomach.

"But if it means you want to explore the thoughts that are making you blush?" Chela added. "I'm betting there's a lovely room at the top of these stairs that was designed just for me, so you know where I am if you decide that."

For a moment, the bluntness of the Hound left Aislinn

silent, but then she straightened her shoulders and said, "There is. A room, I mean."

"Show me."

Aislinn's voice was breathy as she echoed, "Show you . . .?"

"Whatever you want." Chela's hand dropped. She stepped around Aislinn and bounded up the stairs. Her voice filtered down the stairwell. "No requirements, Ash. No anything. Just an open door if you decide to act on it."

By the time the Summer Queen had her expression under control, she'd started up the stairs and made it almost to the top floor. She made a mental note that she was only breathless from the exhaustion not from Chela's words, but lies weren't the domain of faeries. Aislinn could only think that in the privacy of her own mind and even then, as a question.

Mortal hang-ups about propriety clouded Aislinn's mind, and threaded through them was the fact that Seth undoubtedly already saw this potential future thread. His future-seeing was sometimes more frustrating than his months upon months of absence. He was gone half of every year, away in Faerie with the High Queen, and then when he was here in the regular world, he traveled all the time seeing to the needs of the Solitary Faeries.

And I am left alone.

Untouched.

Unloved.

It was no wonder that the thought of uncomplicated affection had her heart all aflutter, and her body whispering, "Why not?"

Chela stood at the wall that had been removed and replaced with a window. It was one of the few major renovations Aislinn had done up here. The entire living room wall was gone, and in its place was a wall of glass. The center of that glass wall opened to the fresh air, and a balcony woven of the branches of a nearby tree leaned against the building.

"Ani and Tish, Gabriel's daughters, used to talk about hating to feel trapped," Aislinn said. "Ani was worse, and she was more Hound than human. So I thought you might feel that same way."

Chela nodded, staring out at the park where Summer held revels and danced.

Aislinn had thought Chela might like the view, but now she was doubting herself. "If you hate it, I can—"

"It's perfect." Chela stepped outside, hands holding the branches lightly. "Could use a few flowers, but aside from that, it's perfect."

With a wave of her hand, Aislinn pulled the deep red clematis blossoms and green vines upward until they were here at the top of the building. Silently, she summoned them to wrap around the branches, as if the living balcony was a trellis. In the next few moments, the Hound was surrounded by a bower of blossoms.

"Exactly like that." Chela glanced over her shoulder at Aislinn. "You are kinder to us than the Dark was. They acted as if the Hunt was still Gabriel's, as if nothing had changed. Irial sometimes called me 'Gabe' as if I was the same person, as if *I* had been his companion for all these centuries. I was not. I was the second in command, the one who managed the Hunt when Gabe and Iri went off on their travels. I was the one who kept things steady when Gabe was managing the Dark King's moods over whichever lover had spurned him."

Aislinn stared at her, realizing again that there were parts of the fey's near-eternal lives that she simply couldn't fathom.

"That was *his* court of choice. I am the Gabriela, and the Hunt is shaped at my will now." Chela looked vaguely terrifying, as if the fear that roiled inside the Hunt was something she could summon. "I will set my path, just as he set his, and to do that, I will live here with your flowers and your hunger for blood. It is not enough to take the lead. I want to state my independence from the past, Ash. I want to claim power."

And *that* was something Aislinn understood completely.

"So let the Dark come. Let Winter come. I give you my allegiance, Summer Queen. And woe to anyone who thinks they can question the choices of the Gabriela." Chela's voice was growing louder, and from the park, the Hunt started seething toward the building.

Her words were a growl as she yelled, "We make our home *here*."

The building shook as they filled it with their thunder and fear and hunger. And Aislinn pulled earth and rock to buttress the shaking walls. She would shelter them, and they would be the force of her will in the world.

"To power," Aislinn said quietly. She opened a bottle of Summer Wine she'd left on the kitchen counter. "To our alliance."

Chela watched her pour wine into a glass, but instead of accepting the glass, the Hound took the bottle. She clinked it gently against the glass Aislinn was holding and added, "To power. To our alliance. And to taking what we want when the time is right."

Aislinn felt her cheeks burn at the layers of meaning there, but she echoed, "To taking what we want."

And she watched Chela drink sunlit wine as if she had always been a part of Summer. Had her vow been untrue, that wine would not leave the Hound with the wide grin now on her lips.

"To a beautiful Summer," Chela added then.

And this time, Aislinn did not blush.

There would be consequences, but in this moment, the Summer Queen found that she didn't care at all. She had expanded Summer's land, expanded her power, and a deadly, beautiful woman was sharing summer wine with her.

So what if the other courts objected?

Chapter Twenty-Eight

KATHERINE

"This is a terrible idea," Katherine said again. She looked down at the world, swallowing against the twist in her stomach. She had expected to be somewhere with Urian tonight, maybe an indulgent hotel where they would order room service and spend the night in silk sheets or whatever luxury hotels were like. She honestly wasn't even sure—but that was what she planned to figure out tonight.

Not how to face a faery queen or ride a dragonish creature. This felt like a fever dream or nightmare, not the happy fantasy she'd fully intended to enjoy that night.

The shape-of-creature that Callisto was right now said nothing. She made a growling grumbling noise a few times, but that wasn't exactly a conversation. Honestly, going to Faerie was the *only* idea that made any sort of sense.

What else was there to do?

Katherine had been pondering the options as Callisto flew—but there weren't many choices. Katherine couldn't go home and risk the Hunt coming for her mother and aunt. She couldn't go up against them by herself and have any real hope of rescuing Urian. And honestly, she couldn't just try to hide. No one could hide from the Hunt.

So that left going to Faerie.

The mere thought of it made Katherine want to puke. Who went to the place where their sort was imprisoned? Who willingly chose the path she was on?

A lovesick fool, that's who.

The thought of abandoning Urian wasn't even worth considering. She hadn't ever believed in love at first sight, or soulmates, but he was hers. She knew that as surely as she knew that he'd come for her if she'd been taken by the Hunt.

The only female gancanagh.

Maybe it was why he loved her. Maybe she loved him, in part, because he was a *gancanagh*. The *why* of the thing didn't matter. Love was love, and regardless of what "caused" it, love was worth risks.

Or going into the lair of an enemy.

Katherine wished she knew more about the courts, the regents, all of it. She'd lived in fear so long that she felt completely unprepared. All she could say so far was that the landscape of Faerie looked a lot like a fairy tale forest. Trees stretched up tall enough that Callisto's belly might brush against them. And the undergrowth was sparse in places, like paths were carved through the wooded area. A river sliced through the whole of it, and creatures roamed.

When Callisto landed on a mossy patch of ground that was akin to a meadow but without the waving grasses, Katherine was hesitant to climb down.

Callisto solved that by switching back to her human shape, which sent Katherine tumbling to the moss-covered ground.

"We walk now." Callisto was still holding Katherine's suitcase, and she strolled off with it.

"Walk *where?*"

"To see the people." Callisto kept going, headed toward a cottage that Katherine hadn't noticed. She didn't slow or speed, just steadily loped over the ground in a walk that seemed less human than even her appearance.

"Which people?"

"Hound," Callisto said.

"Like in the Hunt?" Katherine paused. "Wait! I thought I was *hiding* from them."

Callisto snorted. "Walk."

Katherine wasn't sure that this was a better or worse idea. She trusted Urian, so she'd been trusting Callisto by extension. Was that a mistake? She thought about what she knew—Callisto was a car that was fey and apparently also had a human shape. All else she knew was that the fey couldn't lie directly.

"Can I trust you?" Katherine asked bluntly. "Do you mean me harm?"

At that, Callisto stopped and pivoted. "I want you to help Uri. I mean you no harm. You are his mate. Mates *matter.*"

Then she was off again, and this time, Katherine hurried to keep up with her.

When they reached the house, Callisto opened the door and went inside. The two people there seemed utterly unsurprised by this. The man, who looked like he had hair made of tinsel that was reflecting countless holiday lights, looked up and nodded. He was . . . stiff. There was likely a better word for it, but it was as if he was barely moving. Formal in a way that made him look inhuman. No fey that she'd ever seen looked like this.

Old. He was old. Ancient was a more likely answer, and with age came a stillness. She shouldn't feel surprised. This *was* Faerie. Who knew what oddities thrived here.

The woman, whose hair was pink tipped and longer on the front and one side than in the back, grinned. "What are *you* doing here, Cally? How?"

"The Hunt took Urian. This is his mate." Callisto shoved Katherine forward so suddenly that she stumbled. Then she dropped Katherine's suitcase, which made a clunking noise. "I broke a door to enter."

"They took *Urian*?" The man moved, coming to his feet without seeming to actually move visibly. It was unsettling, like watching a statue shift in front of her. He was somehow already at the door then. He said, "I will tell my sister. She likely knows, but one can never tell with her assorted foundlings."

Then, with another dip of his head to them, he exited. Callisto flashed a grin at them and followed him.

And Katherine was left alone with a stranger.

"I'm Ani," the woman said. She was everything opposite the ancient faery, seeming very human, especially in contrast to him. "*That* was Devlin. Be welcome in our home, mate of Urian."

"Katherine." She folded her arms over her chest, as if she could hold herself steady and stop her fears. "I'm not sure what's going on here. Are you?"

"The Hunt, my family of a sort, has taken your mate, who happens to be like a beloved nephew to the first faery—Sorcha. She's the High Queen." Ani sighed, blowing her hair up in the process and looking disarmingly like a little girl about to pout. "Moody and unpredictable, but fortunately she's trapped here in Faerie. On the *other* hand, Urian's dad is Irial, the former Dark King and current embodiment of Chaos. The Hunt is not really a *part* of the Dark Court, but sort of. They stay with the Dark. And the last time Niall—that's the current Dark King—and Irial were at odds, Niall and the Summer and Winter Courts were all caught up in a war. In other words, this is . . . *bad*."

Katherine blinked, trying to make sense of the things Ani was saying.

"Guess he didn't go over his whole family tree?" Ani snorted. "Men."

"I knew his father was a king, but that's a lot. Any other details I ought to know?" Katherine said, not actually expecting any.

"Uri's niece is the Summer Queen." Ani shrugged.

At that, Katherine started to feel faint. "He said he was an exiled prince . . . but I guess I thought . . . I mean, not that it was a lie, but like he was a bastard son of some lesser someone. Not really legitimate claims to two thrones."

"Nope. Urian's pedigree is obnoxiously valid." Ani rolled her eyes. "And he's obnoxious. No offense."

Katherine stared at her. "I feel completely at a loss here. Callisto—who until yesterday I thought was just a car—said the Hunt took him and they had my scent, so I had to hide."

"Sex is hard to resist with a *gancanagh*." Ani nodded. "I mean, I had no issue resisting Urian because he's a brat, but his dad . . ." She lowered her voice. "It's not a thing I mention in front of Dev, but . . . Iri was *tempting* when I came of age."

.　.　.

"Isn't he . . . old?"

Ani laughed. "You mean experienced? Yes. I might not *like* Urian, but I understand him. A *gancanagh's* touch addicts mortals. Mine drains them. The cost for them is ultimately the same. It takes a strong faery to keep me content. Luckily, Dev is even . . . you know, *older* than Iri."

"Dev is . . . ?" Katherine gestured to the door.

"Yep. Him. He's my husband? Mate? Whatever the term you use is," Ani said. "My heart beats in his body, you know?"

Katherine nodded. "Right. And Iri is . . .?"

"Irial. Urian's dad."

"Urian hates him," Katherine said quietly.

"Oh, sure. He blames him for everything. Totally not accurate, but . . ." She shrugged. "What can you do? Not my circus, not my monkeys, right? Although I guess if you're his mate, it's your circus now, huh? Good luck with that."

Katherine walked over to a table. "May I?"

"Oh shoot! Yes. I should've said that. Have a seat. Food? Liquor? Tea?" Ani came forward. "I'm shit at this part. Dev's all manners and stuff. I'm more . . ." She shrugged, but she was smiling when she said, "I useful in a fight. Loyal. You know, basic Hound stuff."

Katherine took a teacup, and Ani poured fresh tea in it.

"I'm not sure what I'm to do," Katherine admitted. "I don't know who has him or where. I don't exactly feel capable of fighting kings either, but . . . I can't abandon him or hide from the Hunt forever."

Ani gave her a pat on the hand.

"Callisto knows more than I do, though, and she brought me to you." Katherine peered at the other girl. "Hound. As in you are part of the Hunt?"

Ani nodded. She made a face.

"So you left the Hunt?" Katherine guessed.

"Not quite . . ." Ani looked at the door. "My, err, father was Gabriel. *The* Gabriel. Leader of the Hunt."

"Of course, he was," Katherine muttered. "So you, what? Can put in a good word?"

"Not exactly . . . his mate took over after Gabriel died, and you know . . . he wasn't exactly *faithful* to her. My mom was human." Ani held her gaze. "Not that there was anything wrong with that!"

"My mom's human," Katherine said quickly. "Dad was a *gancanagh*."

"So you're . . ." Ani stared, but she didn't continue speaking, just stared in a weird kind of awe.

"A *gancanagh*. Yeah."

"But you're female!" Ani stood and leaned forward, sniffing deeply. "Holy fuck. You're a *gancanagh*. So you and Uri are like fate and stuff. His dad will be so thrilled!"

"Okaaay . . . ?"

"I bet Sorcha already knows, so she'll help. Gah. There will be a fight. This is awesome. I can't imagine Niall sending the Hunt, but I'd love to have an excuse to—"

"Aislinn sent them," Devlin said, returned from wherever he had been so quietly that Katherine only knew he was there when he spoke. "The Summer Queen sent the Hunt."

"*Ash?*"

Devlin nodded. "My sister has allowed you or I to go with the girl. Not both." He paused. "Balance cannot be absent from Faerie. If you'd rather, I can go. I am more--"

"Diplomatic? Or more capable of fighting?" Ani grinned.

"I shall not debate which of us is more adept in a fight, but diplomacy . . ." He gave her a look that made Katherine think she best look away.

But instead of swooning, Ani let out a chortle. "I might not be a diplomat, but *one* of us is more welcome in the Dark Court, and it's not you, love."

He nodded. "I will expect your safe return."

The words sounded less like politeness than an order, but now, Ani did look swoony-eyed. She went up onto her tiptoes and pressed her lips to his. A visible prism of energy flooded the room. Ani tensed, and in that moment, she looked so much like Callisto that it hit Katherine.

Callisto is a Hound.

"Always, my love. Always," Ani whispered. "They can burn the world, and I'd still come home to you."

And Katherine felt both awkward and like she had learned more about the world of faeries in the last two days than in her whole life.

"Let me grab some weapons!" Ani trilled as she darted away. "I haven't seen anyone over there in *years*. This is awesome!"

Katherine looked at Devlin. "Is Callisto . . . like Ani? And what was . . . why is Ani . . . *giddy?*"

"Ani was a child of the Dark Court," he said by way of explanation. "So she misses them. And the Summer Queen was her friend."

"But if the Summer Queen is the one who has Urian . . ."

Devlin gave her an openly sympathetic look. "The courts are complicated, child. Urian had to have done something to anger Summer, but if the Dark and Sunlight are at odds, Ani will pick the darkness. Loyalty is everything in a Hound."

"And you?"

He flashed a rather terrifying smile. "Depends on which path is most advantageous. My loyalty is to Ani, Rae, and Faerie."

"Rae?"

"Long story," Ani said as she came in with a clattering bag of weapons. "Do you need a sword? Mace? You don't really look like a poleax kind of woman. . ."

And all Katherine could do was nod, because she was more confused than not. "Swords are nice. Dagger? I have some weapons in my bag, though. Steel blades."

Ani let out a low whistle, and at the same time, Devlin started, "Ani . . . if she . . ."

"I know, love. I got this."

Despite the apparent oddity of their relationship, the quieter faery nodded. "If you prefer."

She looped an arm around Katherine. "So Urian's mate likes closer combat. Makes a weird sense. We ought to also pack some wounders. Not so much with the steel, right? Wounders are the thing. Not as fatal, but it hurts like it will be."

"Not fatal?" Katherine echoed.

Ani nodded. "We live for ages, Kat. Can I call you Kat? It's funny, right? The Hound and the Kat . . . We're going to have fun. I've never really had a girls' weekend."

"Girls . . ." Katherine looked over her shoulder at Devlin, who was no longer looking their way.

"They're a thing in books. Go away, refresh and recharge." Ani clapped her hands. "Let me get you a little armor, too. Come on!"

Katherine wasn't sure how she felt about any of this, and no one answered her question about Callisto—who was now missing.

But there was something about Ani that she liked instinctively, and for that, Katherine was grateful. Maybe being brought to Faerie wasn't the worst thing ever.

Chapter Twenty-Nine

URIAN

When Urian woke, he was fairly certain a desert had crawled into his mouth, blood and dirt, dry and bitter. he would've begged for water if he were the begging sort. He was manacled in what looked like a stable. Straw covered the floor. The restraints on his wrists and ankles were attached to chains that allowed him to slump on that straw-covered ground.

Urian pushed to his knees, studying his surroundings. A trough of water was in reach. No food. It wasn't food he wanted, though. He vaguely recalled running behind the Hunt. The dirt and dust from their hooves was what he breathed. No wonder that he was parched now.

Cautiously, Urian crawled toward the trough.

"I should've known you were out there in the world," Irial's voice came from the shadows. "I apologize for my absence."

Urian paused. Bloody, clothes in tatters, and crawling wasn't how he'd ever pictured meeting *him*.

Urian scoffed despite everything. "You figured *that* out finally. Wouldn't mom be impressed . . ."

Irial stepped forward, not too close but no longer hiding in shadows.

Urian had managed to avoid meeting him for over a century, but that didn't make it any easier to look at him now. They shared enough features that Urian could almost call the older faery a mirror. Urian was not as dark-of-complexion, and he thought his own voice was less of a drawl than the monster's, the one who'd ruined Urian's mother's life. There was no denying the resemblance, though.

"I had no idea, or I would've come to her," Irial added. "I didn't even know you existed until recently, son. The curse—"

"Not your son, Irial." Urian spat the words, but they sounded rawer than he liked. A mouthful of dirt wasn't doing his voice any favors. "Fucking my mother doesn't make you a fa—"

A slap rocked Urian's head back and stole his words. He fell backward on the cold ground.

"Don't speak of her that way," Irial said, looming over him now and looking every bit the monster in Urian's nightmares even as he swore, "I loved Thelma. I will *always* love her."

"Sure looked that way when she wasted away dreaming of you." Urian lifted his head to stare up into those too-familiar eyes. "She believed you'd return even on her dying day. She died with your name on her lips, dreaming of you, and *you weren't there.*"

Irial looked like he'd been struck. "To protect her, to protect my children, I was cursed to forget her and you."

Urian rolled his eyes. "I heard about it, old man. I know. Loved us enough to leave us. You're the original deadbeat dad. My heart breaks for y. . ." Urian shook his head. "You know what? I can't even say it with sarcasm. I have nothing to say to you."

He shook his arms so the chains that stretched across the floor made a rattling noise. "You got what you wanted. You met me. Now, let me go."

Irial shook his head. "I can't."

"What? Say whatever else you want, but *let me go*." Urian pushed himself back to his feet, swaying slightly. "You want to be a father? Set me free before they get here."

Irian's jaw tightened.

"Look. I get it. You made your excuses to me, and I heard you out. Prove you *really* give a fuck. Set me free." Urian swallowed to keep his still-dry throat from hurting. With his so-called father standing there now, Urian was too proud to shove his face into a water trough in front of him.

All Urian wanted was to get back to Katherine. A terrifying thought hit him then.

"Was anyone else brought in?" he asked quietly. "With me?"

Irial gave him an assessing look. "You know what you are by now. There are consequences to--"

"I'm not out leaving a trail of dead mortals. If that's what you thought, you're wrong." Urian had a flicker of terror.

He wrestled with fears that he couldn't explain.

"Hounds evoke fears," Irial said in barely a whisper. "They're here now."

A voice called out, "I don't think that you were cleared to see the prisoner, Irial."

The Hound stepped into Urian's line of sight, and with

her was Aislinn. The Summer Queen. He'd pissed off the wrong regent, apparently. He'd thought he'd chosen the easier foe, knowing that tangling with the current Dark King and the former Dark King was likely a fool's errand. *For now.* He'd thought the slip of a girl-- barely an adult and recently fey--was the easier target.

"I see that the Hunt has shifted alliances," Irial said before he turned to the Summer Queen. "You carry some of my less charming traits, granddaughter."

"He struck what's mine. And he thinks he's entitled to *my* court," she said with a shrug. There was nothing soft in her. If anything, she looked more intimidating than Irial. She smiled a devastating smile before she challenged Irial, "You would do less when you were king?"

"I never attacked another king's regent—even the kingling. I cursed Keenan, but I didn't have him dragged across the desert like a disobedient dog."

"Well, I suppose that's one for me?" The Summer Queen no longer looked as harmless as she had the first time that Urian had met her. Tendrils of sunlight stretched from her hands like knives, and the head of the Hunt was staring at the diminutive faery queen like she was a blood-dressed goddess.

"The Dark King agreed with my plan, Irial," Aislinn added with a pointed look at Irial. "Is *he* aware that you're here with the prisoner?"

"I am allowed to walk among any court," Irial said mildly. "I don't need his permission."

"Really? I thought he kept you on a fairly short leash these days . . ."

At the hurt that flashed in Irial's eyes, Urian wondered if he'd been wrong about who was the actual monster.

"Does Niall know the Hunt has come to your court?" Irial asked. "They rarely depart the Dark for any other court."

The Hound at the Summer Queen's side shrugged. "I'm sure he'll figure it out eventually. The Hunt is no court's property, Irial."

Then Irial stepped close enough to the Summer Queen that the head of the Hunt looked poised for violence.

"You're my *family*, Ash, but *he* is, too." Shadows lashed out like solid bars and created a cage around Urian, shielding him from harm. "Don't ask me to choose between you. Please?"

For a moment, no one spoke.

Then the Summer Queen sighed. "You are not a king, Irial. And even if you were, I answer to no man, no regent. I've never had a father or grandfather. I have no husband. I have no regent to whom I swore fealty. Ever." She shook her head. "Nothing. No man. No cause. *Nothing* is more important than the safety of my court. And this man"—she pointed at Urian—"hurt one of my advisors."

"He's young—"

"You want me in your life, grandfather? Don't forget who I am. Don't mistake our exchanges of affection for the idea that you can order me *in any way*."

Then her sunlit gaze turned to Urian and the cage of shadows around him evaporated.

"You are charged with threatening the Summer Court, Urian." She paused. "You will stand trial for this offense. If you are found to be a threat that must be nullified, a sentence will be handed down."

Several Hounds appeared then and surrounded Irial.

"Until your trial, you will remain here in seclusion."

Aislinn glanced at the head of the Hunt. "He is not to have *any* unsupervised visitors."

Then she turned and walked away as a crush of Hounds created a wall between Urian and Irial. They faced Irial, clearly seeing him as the only real threat. Urian was in chains, weak, and exhausted.

And all Urian could do was look at the former Dark King. Irial was motionless, and Urian swallowed whatever pride he still had.

"Katherine of Miller," he mouthed. "Protect her. Please . . .*father.*"

Urian wasn't at all sure that the faery saw—or cared. Urian wasn't willing to beg for himself, but he was willing to do whatever it took to keep Katherine safe.

"Tell me what you want," he called out. "Summer Queen! Ash! Tell me what vow you want!"

No one answered.

And then, Irial turned and walked away, escorted out by at least ten Hounds.

Chapter Thirty

AISLINN

Of all the things she thought Seth would say the next morning, nowhere on the list was, "We need to go to Faerie. Now."

"Seth . . ." She blinked her eyes. This wasn't the plan she'd had for morning. Several months of his absence while she was untouched, alone, and missing him made her unwilling to do anything but be here naked with him.

"Trust me on this one," he said. "I trust *you*, Ash. On everything. On the things you've done that scared me, of co-ruling a court with another man—"

"Not fair!" she interrupted. "He had the court first and—"

"I *trust* you," Seth repeated, pulling her toward the ground, tumbling them out of the bed in her room that was currently dangling from the ceiling from a tangle of vines.

She looked over the edge as he half-leaped to the floor. Looking up, he added, "And I trust you not to give away all of your heart if you get . . . interested in someone when I'm away in Faerie."

"My heart is yours," she swore.

"I know. Right now, that's truth." He caught her as she leaped down. Admittedly, she would've been fine anyhow, but she liked that he did so all the same. "But the Summer Court—in its entire history—has never had a monogamous regent until the last few years."

"I know." She looked away, embarrassed at the direction the conversation had gone.

"Summer is a time of pleasure, of joy, of languid days naked and satisfied," he told her, pulling her gaze back to him.

"So . . ." She motioned to the bed they'd just vacated. "Why can't we stay here? Do just that?"

Seth gave her a patient look. "Because I'm *not* Summer, Ash. In order to be fey at all, I have obligations that . . . I need to go, and she wants you to come this time. I can't make you, but I'm *asking* you to come with me because I'm going."

Aislinn looked around the room, hating the flicker of apprehension she felt at the thought. Her court was where she belonged. That was unchanging, but he'd never forced the matter.

"And if I asked you to stay?"

Seth grabbed her and kissed her like he would suffocate her, and within a few moments, she realized that she'd begun tugging him into a bower of flowering vines again.

"Please don't. I'll be here later," he promised.

And Aislinn pouted at the refusal. There was a hunger that embarrassed her since realizing that his logical side wasn't always willing to frolic as she wanted. She didn't love him any less than when she was mortal. If anything, she loved him more, but she had more than a few moments of resenting the things that pulled him away from her. A flicker of awareness washed over her that he knew that, and it was why he was, in essence, giving her permission to be . . . more like the rest of court. She just wasn't sure how she felt about that. What she'd wanted was for him to give her more of his attention, not suggest she . . . outsource her needs.

But that wasn't what she wanted to deal with right now. She pulled away from Seth and said, "So you can hear her in your head now?"

"Mother? Yeah. She summons me sometimes." He shrugged like it wasn't a big deal that another regent called him away from her, that he was not bothered at all by it.

"And you still do favors for Niall, too?" she murmured.

"Ash?"

"I can't, Seth. I can't deal with the fact that I keep losing swaths of your time for them." Aislinn stepped back. "I'm not saying never, but I'm not coming with you. I have a trial to handle, a prisoner to see to, and there are new building plans for the adjacent block."

"The adjacent block?"

"I bought it." She pulled a dress over her head and left the room, calling back, "I guess I'll see you when you pencil me in again."

When she walked away, she hated that her tears were making the entire loft fill with a rainstorm. The door to the bedroom slammed closed as Seth left, so she knew he was going.

A part of her hoped he'd follow.

A part of her whispered that she could follow.

But most of her knew that he was not wholly hers. It

wasn't that she wanted a consort like Donia had—or two like Niall had. She simply wanted to be the regent who held his loyalty, and it felt more and more like Sorcha beckoned him whenever she wanted. It was no longer the few months of time they'd agreed to in order for him to be a faery.

Was it so wrong to want to be the most important faery in his life? Was it so wrong that he be there for her more than when he found the time? It wasn't just about the sex. It was about wanting to share dances, meals, lazy mornings, to tell him about her day, and to spend her nights in his arms.

Five years, and they were still where they'd been as teenagers.

Keenan was willing to let the world burn for Donia.

Niall all but burned it down for Irial.

Devin created a new court to be with Ani.

Why couldn't she have that same sort of devotion?

Chapter Thirty-One

KATHERINE

Being brought to Faerie was, in fact, the worst thing ever. Before they could head off to the world to rescue Urian, Callisto said, "One quick stop."

"I don't have time to—"

"Nonnegotiable. Rules are rules." Then she twisted her fingers into Katherine's in a childish handholding. "Can we skip?"

"No."

Callisto looked at Ani. "You?"

Ani took Callisto's other hand in hers, and they skipped. Katherine walked, faster than normal to keep up with the skipping faeries.

Next lesson. They're all a little bonkers.

Katherine had a stray thought that she and Urian would need to talk about normal life before they ever had a kid.

She stumbled at that thought. *Kids?* She wasn't sure he was even still alive. "What if he's dead?"

Callisto squeezed her hand. "He's not."

"How can you know that? He could—"

"Prisoner at the Summer Queen's home," Callisto said. She gave an exaggerated face-scrunched up sniff. "I can sniff him out."

A wave of fear fell away from Katherine. "What did he say? How is he?"

Anything else she could have said faded away as a man stepped from nothing into existence.

"Doorway," Callisto whispered.

Ani screamed and launched herself at the intruder.

And Katherine drew a knife with her free hand, eying the intruder. He was . . . an older version of Urian in face and form, but he looked like he shopped at a shop catering to rock stars and billionaires. She might not have money, but a lifetime in seclusion gave a woman a *lot* of time to read online catalogues and celebrity magazines.

"Iri!" Ani cried as the man caught her mid-leap and spun her around in the air like she was a small child.

"Pup." He looked at Katherine and Callisto as he lowered Ani back to the ground. "Introduce me?"

Ani gave him a look. "As if you don't know . . ."

"Irial, right?" Katherine said, not stepping forward or lowering her blade. "Were you involved in Urian's capture?"

"Inadvertently." He looked poised even as she took several steps forward. "But I spoke to him . . . and when I returned, I met a lovely young steed"—he gestured at Callisto—"who suggested I visit Faerie."

Callisto giggled. "I remember when we roamed, Dark King of Before."

She appeared to be acting coquettishly. She tilted her head and held out some sort of fat, dead lizard. "Fed you and the scarred one. Watched you . . ."

Irial bowed his head. "Being near wild magic is always an honor, Callisto."

"I raised your pup as well as I could," she said softly. "Took him to see the best sex workers, great art, museums, read to him when Tam was napping, and he slipped out of the house."

Irial nodded. "Would that I could have looked after him myself. . ."

Katherine cleared her throat loudly. "Can we reminisce or whatever when he's not imprisoned? And why"—if you both saw him—"did you not just set him free?"

Callisto laughed. "You are a good mate."

"What's say that we slip away before we have to involve Sorcha?" Ani suggested, voice barely a whisper now. "She's not terribly fond of Ash as it is. Bad enough that Seth spends so much time with her, but now she's captured Uri?"

Irial made a sweeping gesture, and a silver fold of air appeared. Katherine had seen it when she entered Faerie, but it was different to see it up close.

They stepped forward, and in the next moment, they were stepping out of the veil-like doorway. It seemed to reseal with a slithering sensation, as if it truly were some sort of multi-hued fabric.

Katherine jabbed her hand toward where the veil was, but there was nothing there.

"You can't cross the veil without permission from both courts in Faerie," Ani said.

"Or be Chaos," Irial said.

"Or wild magic," Callisto said.

"So how . . ." Katherine looked around at them: one former Dark King who was now Chaos, one wild magic in whatever shape she chose, and Ani. "What are you?"

"Errr, Shadow Queen, so you know, Dev asked his sister —the High Queen—and she said one of us could go," Ani looked remarkably sheepish.

"Right, well, I can't deal with"—Katherine waved her hand at the lot of them—"any of you right now. I just want to see Uri."

"We can fight our way in!" Ani said in a far too cheerful voice. "Maybe not you, Iri? Can't imagine that going too well . . ."

And though Katherine didn't know Irial, she could see Urian in his expression as he weighed the merits of what he was doing. There was likely no one there that thought he was making a wise choice as he said, "The wolves still around, pup?"

Ani sort of shivered, and a growling noise filled the air— like bees but far, far louder. Her tattoos, almost all of wolves, seemed to be moving. The creatures' red eyes gleamed so brightly that it was as if the whole of the woman was illumi- nated in red.

Then in a chaotic blur, wolves seemed to materialize. It was as if the ink jumped off her body and before it hit the earth, it shifted into a massive wolf-like creature.

Muzzles and tails, bone and blood, fear and muscle, each creature took form. Then they were suddenly surrounded by growling, red-eyed wolves the size of small horses.

Katherine wasn't sure whether to be terrified or excited. She'd gone from "not in this world" to right in the heart of faery troubles.

They were a few blocks from where Urian was being held when Irial paused mid-step. "He asked for you."

Katherine nodded.

"I *do* want to come with you. I'll attract enemies, though, so tell him . . . just tell him I came?" He looked less like the walking temptation that he'd appeared to be—not that she was tempted, but she *got* it. He was an older version of Urian. Beautiful. Deadly.

"If you do this, Niall will be furious." Ani nudged him with her shoulder. "Just wait at the Crow's Nest or something. I'll bring him to you."

Then a scream of rage rocked them all back. Whatever caused that pain wasn't a thing she wanted to face.

But there wasn't much of choice now, for any of them. The wolves were running, and Ani ran with them. Irial and Katherine were both swept up in the race of fur and teeth.

No words. No hesitation.

Please let him be alive.

Chapter Thirty-Two

AISLINN

From the comfort of her loft, the Summer Queen watched her beautiful garden fall to ruins from ice and shadows. Whatever else she was expecting today, this wasn't it. She felt Winter Court and Dark Court in her domain, and a rage built in her skin that made her wonder if peace was at its end.

This is why Seth wanted me to walk away. To come to Faerie.

"My queen?" Tavish was at her side, as ever. And Siobhan was at her other side.

"I suspect they realized that we are holding Urian," Aislinn said lightly.

"Son of the Summer and the Dark," Tavish said, "I cannot fathom why they'd be concerned."

Aislinn realized that her entire body glowed brighter than any but her own court could face, and there was no way to safely go to the park and negotiate when she was akin to a small star in that moment. "I expected Niall to let me handle this. He knew I was—"

"He knew you were *borrowing* the Hunt, Ash. He's likely

here to try to suggest that you've mis-stepped." Chela seemingly materialized out of nothing, but after a startled moment, Aislinn realized that she'd simply been running faster than sight.

"Oh." Aislinn tried to pull the heat back into her skin. How the Hunt would respond to such things was unclear.

But Chela lifted Aislinn's glowing hand to her lips. Her breath was a welcome chill as she swore, "My fealty to Summer."

"I know. You don't need—"

"I fight, so you do not need to." Chela turned Aislinn's hand over and kissed her palm, searing her lips in the process, and then she was gone as quickly as she'd arrived.

Any guilt Aislinn had in the fact that she'd burned the other woman's lips vanished under the comfort in having someone at her side. *I'm not alone figuring this out.* She had been when the courts were at the edge of war a few years ago. She'd had advisors, fighters, but she was ultimately the one making the decisions.

A queen without a consort.

More and more Aislinn wasn't pleased with that reality, but she didn't feel as alone as she watched the Hunt pour into the already ruined garden like a dark swarm. Hooves and talons ripped furrows in the earth. Growls and thuds punctuated the slivery sound of swords.

"My queen?" Tavish prompted.

"Mmmm?" Aislinn watched the crush from a window in the loft.

"Orders?" Siobhan asked.

"Stay here. There is no need for my court to fight. It's a . . . statement that we do not." Aislinn decided with a nod to herself. "Let the Hunt clarify their loyalty."

"And the Winter?" Siobhan kept pace with her as Aislinn headed toward the balcony.

That was another matter entirely. Aislinn had trusted Keenan, spoke freely to him and now he was here. In her home. He ought to know better. He ought to know that bringing the ice to this place, to this court, was not a thing to do lightly. He knew better than most how the Summer Court had suffered under the reign of Winter in the past centuries.

"Stay here," Aislinn repeated as she stepped onto her balcony. "Fighters would be an acknowledgment of war. This is simply saber rattling."

Then she stepped off the ledge and used sunlight to create a glowing staircase to descend into the fracas. It was showy, arrogant, and—as far as she was concerned—a statement that needed making.

The Winter King, the former Summer King, was trying to convince the Hunt to let him pass. In his rage, frost and snow were falling on Summer's domain.

"I don't recall a meeting on my schedule," Aislinn said lightly as she walked down the remaining sunlit steps.

As she intended, Keenan turned to look at her. "Winter has a right to interrogate the prisoner. He's a threat to—"

"My court." Aislinn strode toward him, her every step melting the ice he'd dared to spread on her ground. "*Mine*, Keenan. My court. My prisoner. My relative, in fact. You dare to come here with this"—she gestured at the snowfall around him—"as if you have rights *here*?"

"Now, Ash—"

She let out a growl. "Do you declare war on Summer? Invading my territory? What were you thinking?"

Plants exploded on either side of her, and the soil under her feet started to boil.

Louder, she repeated her question. "Do you declare war on Summer? Invading my territory? What were you thinking?"

Her voice resonated like she was the thunder in the clouds she was summoning to her bidding.

"If you are not of my court, or of the Hunt, you better have a damn good explanation for being here," she thundered. "Do not mistake *my* Summer Court for the"—she flashed teeth at Keenan—"more *impotent* one that you are used to seeing these last centuries."

Keenan held her gaze but said nothing.

"Go," she said. "I will not forgive this. I'm sick of everyone underestimating me. I'm not a child, not a mortal, not the 'young queen.' I'm your fucking equal, Keenan. Summer balanced Winter, and you forget yourself coming here as if you have *rights* to speak to my guest. If you test me again, you won't like the result."

Then she stepped around him. Her guards and the Hounds parted for her with respect gleaming on their faces, and then they closed formation behind her.

Chapter Thirty-Three

URIAN

The cell where Urian was held was flooding. He'd wanted a drink after he'd been brought here, but now even the trough in his cell was under the floodwater. It was as if a desert monsoon had swept through the building, and the park outside he presumed, and lingered.

The muddy mess was up to his shins when he woke a few moments ago, and if it continued much longer, he would be forced to consider climbing—assuming he could do that with the chains. There were no guards. For the first time since he'd been here, he was completely alone.

"Hey! I'm in here!" Urian had yelled. "Assholes! I'm not amused right now."

He looked around for ways to get free. The manacles were wrought of thorns and sunlight, and Urian ought to be able to work with that if he had as much affinity for summer as he believed. He wondered if the Summer Queen's choice of restraint was simply a test.

He'd debated altering the manacles. The thorns were his concern. He could make sunlight obey him. It wasn't as easy as shadow, but it was possible. He was not as capable with plants, and the thorns around Urian's wrists were likely to spear his skin if he removed the sunlight. Would the thorns pierce him fatally? Right now, they were simply abrading his skin, but without the sunlight, would they be deadly?

Maybe. But drowning definitely would be . . .

Urian tested the malleability of the sunlight. It was responsive, sluggish but not silent. He weighed the possibility. The water wasn't filling too fast so far, but it was not stopping. And whether it was drip by drip or a surge, it was still adding up.

Then he heard the unmistakable sound of a fight outside.

The water turned to an icy slush. There weren't a lot of guesses as to what that meant: the Winter Court was here.

Urian didn't know whether they were here helping Irial in an ill-fated rescue, or they were here to take him captive, or if it was unrelated to him entirely. But being caught between three courts seemed like a terrible idea.

He shivered, his legs growing numb under the ice water. He shoved his wrists under the water briefly, trying to slow the flow of blood in his veins so that he'd have time to pull the thorns from his skin before bleeding out.

When he heard the roared words of rage from what could only be the Summer Queen, he decided that he'd rather not be trapped no matter who came into the prison.

"Please let this work," he whispered.

Then he drew the sunlight off the manacles into his skin, leaving only the several inch long thorns behind. The plants did not shrink or retract no matter what he willed.

He submerged his wrists again and then raised the thorny restraints to his mouth and began biting and spitting them out. He was tearing flesh from his wrists, and he let out several noises that were sounds he would never admit to making.

But bite by bite, icy water after icy water, he torn them free.

If he'd had another few moments, he'd be free entirely—but then the Summer Queen strode through the flood water. It melted in her path, leaving the room akin to a sauna. Steam rose and curled around her, making her look like a terrible vision of danger headed right toward him.

It took almost every ounce of courage not to step back. It took the last ounce to step toward her. He was only bound by one hand now, but not strong enough to fight her properly. He was losing blood, wavering on his feet from pain, but he let her gaze.

"Niece."

The Summer Queen grabbed him, her hands burning like fire, scorching his skin. He missed the water.

Hell, he wished for ice.

Or to pass out.

"Not the softer regent at all, are you, Ashes?" Urian muttered.

She shoved sunlight toward him like a fist, and without thinking, he pulled shadows from the room and wrapped them around that burning ball of light.

"I don't need a trial to exile you." She glowed like an ancient goddess, and he was, not for the first time, reluctantly impressed by her.

"Then *exile* me. Don't kill me." Urian felt the remaining manacle fall free. A flicker of a thought that he could overcome her rolled through him, but the fact was that he didn't truly want that. He'd hoped to frighten her, to intimidate her, but that clearly hadn't worked.

"For what it's worth," he said, "you're a hell of a queen. I think my mother would've liked you. You're more like her than Moira was, more than Elena in ways . . ."

The Summer Queen stepped back. She stared at him for several moments. "Run, damn it. Stay away from me and mine. Stay away from Seth, from Leslie and Niall. Consider yourself exiled, uncle."

"No love for my father on that list?" Urian said lightly.

She laughed. "He's out there to rescue you." She pointed to the doorway, and he could hear the ruckus outside. "I hate to tell you, but your father is about to have more to worry about than you. . ."

Urian stood staring at her.

"Go before you can't." Aislinn knocked out the wall beside him with a gesture.

Definitely not weak.

"Aren't you *their* queen?"

She gave him a sad smile. "In case you missed the ice, Winter is here. And the Dark decided to make sure they weren't missing a fight. They're both here. Three courts want your blood right now, uncle. Two of them won't listen to me, and I'm not foolish enough to fight them when I can simply set you free."

"I have no words," Urian said, surprised by her candor and the risk she was taking for him. That was what family was.

Then she gave him a hard shove toward the makeshift door and ordered, "*Run.* Don't come back."

Chapter Thirty-Four

KATHERINE

In the distance, she saw Urian—bloody and fighting off what looked like an oversized crocodile.

"It's just a steed," Callisto said, shoving a giant sword into Katherine's hands. "You can use this?"

"Yeah." She took it and started toward him, swinging it in wide arcs with each step.

The montante was a two-handed sword, but longer than the standard longsword. It wasn't quite as awkward to handle as the poleax, but it wasn't a favorite for her. When her mother insisted that Katherine use what was, in essence, spear-clearing sword, Katherine had scoffed. Some day she'd ask more questions about everything her father had told her mother. The preparation that Octavia had given her daughter couldn't be accidental.

"Fuck." Katherine swung the montante sword in a figure-eight pattern that had been awful to learn. She wasn't really tall enough for it, but she was grateful for it in that moment.

To the side, she saw Irial and another man fighting. "Ani? He needs help."

The fierce faery woman laughed as she stabbed a thorn-covered faery in the thigh. She looked toward Urian's father and yelled back, "Nah. That's his worse half. Nothing to be done but stay out of their way."

Katherine wasn't sure she was made for this world.

Irial was on the ground now, and she winced at the other faery slammed what looked like a mallet made of shadows at his leg. Despite everything, she couldn't imagine that he was going to survive.

Then Irial launched himself from the ground like a wave of darkness was propelling him upward. He landed on the other man and wrestled him to the ground. No one went near them. In fact, it was the only vacant part of the now destroyed landscape.

She looked away and ran toward Urian, grateful for the path that Ani's wolves were clearing for her now.

The other faery woman's laughter rang through the yells, and somewhere in the mess of violence, Katherine realized that the Hounds were launching faeries toward Ani like a twisted hockey match.

Then Katherine was somehow already beside Urian. He was bleeding, burned, possibly frost-burned, too. And he looked like he'd topple before long, but he was fighting with a fervor that made her wonder if she was the odd one. Nothing about this seemed like a cause for laughter—but then she realized that he wasn't laughing like Ani.

"Uri!"

He fought his way to her, and then almost as soon as they were side-by-side, they were plucked out of the mass of fighters by what she could best describe as a gryphon. Two clawed feet snatched them up like an eagle plucking a fish from the sea.

Urian thrashed. "Let me d—"

"It's Callisto," Katherine yelled from where she was dangling from another claw. She was fairly sure she was right, although she couldn't say why.

From below her, Ani waved.

Irial stared up at them.

And in a few moments, they were on the ground in a parking lot of what looked like an abandoned shopping mall. Callisto stood there, watching them.

"You'll be able to fly by airplane. She's not going to like it, so hold her hand the whole time to keep her safe from the steel," Callisto said, sounding more coherent than she ever had. "Now that you're free of them, you can't stay on this side of the ocean. No shortcut through Faerie. Go to the Brough House."

Urian looked at her. "I have so many questions."

"If you ask them all, you'll be dead or captive again." Callisto patted his cheek. "Stay on that side of the sea, or you'll die."

Then she looked at Katherine. "I stowed your stuff in Faerie. Shop for something less . . . like my clothes." She grinned. "Then go. I'll take you to the airport, and then I have a debt I must go pay."

Callisto was car-shaped again, almost as soon as the last word was spoken.

"You do that to avoid questions!" Urian shook his head, and then he did some sort of magic that meant that he looked unbruised, and as Katherine looked down, she saw that she looked fine, too.

AISLINN

"What the hell, Irial?" Niall stood over Irial like he was facing a dangerous foe. "Do you ever think about anything but yourself?"

"Niall," Aislinn started as she walked through the ruins of her park to see her grandfather and his beloved arguing. In the way they did everything, their arguing was closer to romance than she could explain.

Irial glanced at her and shook his head once. "I think of you."

"Then you'd stop getting into danger." Niall's abyss guardians lashed out like knives, pinning Irial to the ground. "Keenan still hates you, and that *boy* wants you dead and—"

"I am fine." Irial smiled through a bloody mouth.

"Well, I'm not! I require your presence *and* your safety," Niall said as he punched his beloved.

Irial laughed. "You have them, love."

"I thought I had your *loyalty*, too." Niall growled at his partner and put a boot on his stomach.

And Irial simply grinned. "You want me to retaliate? Or do you want to take this to somewhere more private first?"

"Damn it," Niall muttered. Then he glanced at Aislinn. "*You* might have decided—unilaterally, I might add—to free him knowing he's a danger to my court, but--"

"Declare him heir," Irial suggested from the ground.

Niall swiveled his head and stared at him. "Seriously, Irial?"

"He's my *son,* love. Your stepson in—"

"Was there a wedding I missed?" Niall pulled Irial to his feet and punched him almost in the same moment.

Irial wasn't as quick as Niall with his fists, but he fought with a raw emotion that Niall lacked. Still, eventually, Irial was bleeding on the ground again, and Niall had one boot-clad foot pinning him there. This time, the boot was obviously pressing down.

The former Dark King couldn't open his eyes fully. His lip was cracked. "Do you want to marry me. then? Make an honest man--"

"You don't know when to stop." Niall sighed and looked away. "It's never enough for you. No matter what I give you, no matter—"

"I have a ring, love. Had it for a few centuries now."

Niall looked back down. "*What*?"

As the Dark King started to remove the boot from his beloved's chest, Irial clasped Niall's ankle, keeping him where he was. "I love you. I've loved you for centuries, Niall. You want a public declaration? A ceremony? I'll plan a wedding. One for you and Leslie. One for you and me."

After a moment, Niall asked, "One for you and her?"

"If she'll have me," Irial said lightly.

"So you plot to leave us, return to Faerie for Urian, and

then you *propose*?" Niall stepped back. "It'll take more than a fucking ring to make me forgive that, Iri. You offered to leave me. To leave Leslie."

Irial stayed on the ground. "How did you know?"

Niall looked at Aislinn and then back at Irial. "Seth."

Then he strode away.

Chapter Thirty-Six

KATHERINE

The plane touched down in Scotland with a jolt, and Katherine squeezed Urian's hand in hers. Again. He was her tether on that long flight, as if his immunity to steel had been lent to her by way of his touch. It didn't make sense, but then again, neither did being the son of two courts—or being a female *gancanagh*.

Not shockingly, Urian was still bruised. He hadn't even recovered from being dragged across the country by the Wild Hunt when he'd been held prisoner by an angry queen and fought his way to freedom.

It hadn't even been twenty-four hours, and they were in Europe. They'd put an ocean between them and the angry faery regents.

"Are you okay?" she asked.

They'd flown first class, and it afforded them slightly more privacy, but she was grateful that Urian could don a glamour, hiding the extent of his injuries from the other passengers. He looked like he'd been dragged through rocks and cacti, held up as a punching bag, and that was just the surface stuff. He had multiple broken bones, and the worst thing—oddly perhaps—was that he seemed to have lost some of his spirit, like a mustang recently broken to a saddle.

"She wasn't awful," Urian said. "My niece. I thought she would be . . . but she reminded me of my mother. An angrier version, but still. There's fire in her."

"Literally," Katherine muttered, looking at the burns on his wrist and other hand.

"I liked her." Urian looked like he'd swallowed worms just saying those three words. "And worse . . ."

"What's worse than liking *that* woman?" Katherine had zero love for the woman who had stolen Urian and held him prisoner.

"Irial. I'm worried about him," Urian admitted.

"Fair. I am, too," she whispered. "He went against the Summer and the Dark for you."

"It doesn't fix everything," Urian said quickly.

"Of course."

The seatbelt sign turned off with a chime, and everyone started to stir. Their jeans and shirts looked out of place in the first-class crowd of suits, but Katherine just smiled in a not-too-friendly way. They were mortals, and it was a small space. Having two *gancanaghs* this close had meant that the only time no one was trying to talk to Urian or her was when they'd napped. If she ever wanted a corporate job, she had a stack of business cards, an offer of a villa in Tuscany if they wanted to borrow it, and that was just the less-awkward offers.

"I'm ready to go somewhere with a locked door," she told Urian.

He smiled at her. "Coincidentally, that's where we're going."

They'd traveled without baggage, so as they deplaned, they walked through the airport and waited for the ride Callisto promised.

A steed in the shape of a limo pulled up to the curb. No driver, but as they approached, the back door opened.

Urian waited for her to slide inside, and then he followed. "There's a hotel near Old Town Edinburgh for our sort. No steel. I stayed there for a while . . . It's safe. No court politics allowed inside the grounds. You can dine with members of any court."

"Like in that movie?" She couldn't remember the name, but her mother loved it, mostly because of the fight choreography—at least that was what she said. Katherine couldn't help but notice that the actor looked a lot like her father.

"The one with the faery as the lead actor? Yeah." Urian rolled his eyes. "I don't know how he thinks no one will notice. He doesn't age at all."

Katherine felt foolish for not realizing. It certainly explained how graceful he was. No one that beautiful, that ageless, that graceful could be a mere mortal.

"But yes, like that." Urian pulled her closer. "Do I need to be jealous?"

"Of an actor?" She laughed. "No, well, no . . . unless it'll make you need to remind me why I want you."

This time, Urian gave her a wicked smile. "For days, weeks, months. My only plan is to have you at my mercy."

"Mmmm, tell me more . . ."

The car pulled up in front of what looked like a castle. Towers speared the sky, and an honest-to-goodness moat surrounded the building. Several swans swam in the water, so obviously there was no dragon or monster there.

The building was a dark grey brick, and the drawbridge that they had to cross had brass works rather than steel.

Urian put a hand on the small of her back and directed her across the bridge. At the far side, two guards stood on either side of massive arched wooden doors that looked at least two-feet thick. They looked at Urian with recognition.

One said, "Your father called and asked us to put you on the top floor with guards."

"I'm not interested in a prison," Urian said lightly.

"To make sure you are undisturbed." One guard looked at Katherine. "He also had clothing delivered for both of you." He lowered his voice. "And accessories."

Accessories?

"Silver? Brass?" Urian asked.

"Yes. Steel, as well."

Katherine realized then that they weren't talking about shoes and things of that nature, but weapons. She wished her expression was as unreadable as Urian's, but that was not anywhere in her skill set.

Urian nodded to the guards and led her inside.

The foyer or lobby or whatever the right word was seemed like it was out of a children's film. There was an air of age here, a sort of elegance that ought to be outdated, but instead it looked like a perfectly preserved space. Gemstones and silver and marble created massive art pieces in the floor. It felt criminal to step on it. Behind the lobby clerk was a tapestry that was perfect enough that she expected the unicorns in it to move.

"Sir. Madam. Do you have bags you need brought up to the suite?" The faery was as mundane as any she had seen, looking almost human aside from reptilian eyes.

"We would love a full meal brought up. Champagne,

too." Urian smiled in a way that made it perfectly clear that jeans and a faded shirt made him no less the prince than he was. "No bags, though."

"Very well." The man made a note. "Do you have a flower preference, madam?"

"A what?" Katherine looked at Urian.

"They bring fresh flowers each day," he supplied.

Katherine frowned. "Pass. We want to be undisturbed unless we request something." She wrapped her arm through Urian's. "It's our honeymoon."

A warm smile came over the man's face. "Of course."

Urian glanced down at her then. "Race you? Or carry you?"

She laughed, but as Urian took the key and they got directions to their suite, she said, "If you catch me, you can carry me wherever you want."

Then she took off running.

Urian's laugh was close enough that it would make her run faster if she intended to outrun him, but she didn't really want to win—at least not by outrunning him. She slowed down and waited for him to catch up at the top of the staircase.

There, at the end of a hallway with dark red and gold patterned rug over wooden floors, surrounded by painted wallpaper and lit by old-fashioned oil lights, she paused and met his gaze. "Oh no, I seem to be captured."

"Did you mean it?" he asked.

"That you could carry me?" she teased. "Or that we're on a honeymoon?"

"The latter." He swept her into his arms, and then he strode down the hall as if she weighed nothing.

She rested her head on his shoulder. "This is it for me, Urian. I'm yours."

"For eternity?" He fumbled briefly with the lock, holding her with one arm as he did so.

When the door swung open, she said only, "Yes."

Urian carried her to a bed, which meant walking through the series of rooms that were no doubt opulent, as the rest of the castle was, but she wasn't looking at the rooms. Her full attention was on the man carrying her toward their bed.

"My vow," he said, lowering her to the bed. "My life for yours."

He slid to the floor, so he was kneeling in front of her.

"My vow," she echoed. "My life for yours."

"Unto eternity," he added. "I will love, protect, and cherish you, Katherine of Miller."

She echoed his words and then added, "I love you, Urian. When I thought I lost you, I didn't want to be in the world."

He nodded, understanding in a way that no one else ever could or would. This was the beginning of their forever, and somehow, the few weeks it had taken to get to this point felt too long.

Then he kissed her, sealing the vow, and she felt a sense of completeness beyond anything she could say in mere words. So she said it in the language they would both understand—with kisses and caresses, with moans and begging, with touches and words.

EPILOGUE

Two chairs sat on either side of the divan where the former Dark King now lounged. A second, larger sofa was across from that, and there were two more bookcases. The room was slightly different now that it was Niall's, too, and not just Irial's, but that mostly meant that it was slightly less "decadent bachelor" and slightly more "who reads a lot." Periodically, new works of art cycled in, and others went into storage.

Niall was an art lover, and his beloved was indulgent of pretty much anything that made Niall smile.

He was also the master of artful lounging. The man had perfected the innate sensuality of both the Dark Court and their gancanagh gifts. Niall was prone to violence to repress that side of himself. Irial was prone to . . . decadence.

He lifted a decanter from one of the various alcoves in the wall. He poured amber liquid into a crystal glass and wiggled it like bait. "Drink with me?"

"I'd rather hit you," Niall muttered.

"Flirt." Irial's grin ought not make Niall feel like an unschooled boy, not now, not still. Centuries apart, a few years back together, and still Niall felt like he was a fumbler when it came to the flirtatious side of their relationship.

The abyss-guardians swayed and patted him consolingly. They were his as much as Irial's now, but they'd been an extension of Irial for centuries, so they knew well the frustration of the seemingly indolent former king. That indolence was an act, a façade, though.

When Niall didn't reply, Irial shrugged. He carried the bottle, his half-empty glass, and a second glass over to a low table.

Niall watched. Really, there were things he ought to do, but they needed to resolve this argument—or maybe he was simply as much under the sway of a snake charmer as any other monster.

"Do you suppose there's a way to resolve this?" Irial unbuttoned his shirt and stretched out on the sofa, nearly topless and increasingly languid.

Niall allowed himself to pause and gaze at the invitation, but he didn't give in to the sight. Yet. Softly, he asked, "Do you think that will work on me?"

The former Dark King didn't respond beyond sipping his whisky.

Several moments passed in a silent standoff.

Irial sighed and asked, "Tell me what's wrong."

Niall had been pacing through the house like he only did when he was trying to wrestle with emotions. For all that the Dark Court fed on emotion—the darker sort—Niall still had an excess of discomfort with that part of himself. Now that Irial had him in the study, he'd hoped to redirect that emotional madness toward something mutually rewarding, but now he was wondering if going to the fight ring would have been wiser. Niall was partial to fists to resolve his thoughts.

As if he heard Irial's thoughts, Niall curled his hands into fists at his side. "You cannot expect me to turn around and—"

"Bend to my will?" Irial interrupted.

"Your son tried to *kill* another regent," Niall repeated. "He *hates* you."

"Make him your heir, love. It's not like you have to hand him the court. It's a token, a way to say we accept him, that we want him in our court." Irial caught Niall's hand as he passed by. "Have I ever asked for—"

"You ask for everything." Niall tugged away and sighed. "All the fucking time, Irial."

"Dark Court," Irial said simply, settling back into the cushions to preen a little. The frustration in Niall's voice had been accompanied by his hands unfolding.

Distracted after all.

Niall flopped onto the divan, absurdly beautiful in his temper, and conveniently between the liquor and Irial.

Irial waited to see if Niall was going to do anything.

He offered his glass to Niall, an offering that was not refused this time.

"Can I think about it?" Niall said. "If I agree to that, will you let it go until I—"

"It's your court," Irial said. "I'm a guest in your h—"

Nial snorted. "It's your home, too, but it *is* my court now."

As if it was too much to allow himself to do more, Niall looked at Irial before adding, "I want peace in our home. No matter what I decide. I want *you* here. You and Leslie are my life. I won't invite Urian here, even though he's your son, if he is a threat to either of you."

"That's all I ask. Consider it."

Niall nodded, and then he closed his eyes. Head thrown back, slouched on the sofa like every temptation Irial had ever had to resist.

"Like art," he murmured.

Then Irial made sure his hand landed on Niall's thigh—high enough to be an invitation but not so high as to be presumptuous--as he reached for the second glass. For all the years of loving Niall, Irial never let himself forget that Niall was a gift, a fleeting gift at that, and he could vanish easily the next time Irial fucked up too badly.

"No art," Niall grumbled.

He pulled Irial over him and kissed him. With Irial, Niall kissed the same way he fought—like he wanted to bruise him. The taste of peat smoke on his tongue was as close to heaven as a nightmare could be. Irial was certain of it.

And he wanted more of it.

But the cold chill over his skin made him look over his shoulder. One of the cadaverous Scrimshaw Sisters glided into the room with her usual macabre beauty.

Slowly, careful not to hint at shame or imply rejection, Irial moved off Niall's lap and sat beside him. Niall was not as at ease with the violence of how he loved. To be extra clear, Irial took Niall's hand in his.

Ethereal and vaguely terrifying, the Scrimshaw Sisters were typically Winter Court, but a few had left for the Dark Court when the Winter Queen took a consort they hated.

"Knock first," Irial reminded her. It wouldn't work, but it was always good to at least pretend that he encouraged the Scrimshaw Sisters to follow the rules.

She leaned down and knocked several books to the floor.

"Something like that," Irial muttered. He might be at ease with a lot of things, but the way she stared at his teeth when he talked made him want to be rude. Most faeries would be looking at his bare chest or now too-tight trousers, but that was not of interest to the Scrimshaw Sisters.

"What?" Niall half-snarled, hand tightening on Irial's.

She dropped a piece of shroud on the table, and then drifted away. Irial looked at it while Niall was still glaring at the departing faery.

Irial glanced at the shroud. Written in ashes on the scrap of grave cloth was only: I HAVE LESLIE.

"Niall? Read this."

They exchanged a look, and then Niall was off, calling for guards, for someone to summon the Hunt, for the Scrimshaw Sister to tell him everything.

Irial couldn't move. *Was it Urian?* He'd started to feel like he knew his son, exchange a few coded letters even. If he was wrong, if his trust meant that Leslie was in peril . . .

"Get *up*." Niall grabbed him by the wrists. "Whatever panic you have, it's on hold. Our . . ." He faltered over the word. There was no title for what she was-- Queen? Consort? Heart?—nothing was quite right. Niall shook his head. "Leslie needs us."

Irial picked the shroud up carefully. Any scent on it was their best bet. The Hunt could track the slightest scent.

He looked at the words again: I HAVE LESLIE.

It was as close to a declaration of war as any words could

be. He hoped it wasn't his son, but no matter who it was, this was now *all* that mattered.

The story will continue in
  Wicked Lovely Faery Courts Book 2: Moonlit Stars

lot longer than she'd like. Neither her heart nor her life are safe now that she's juggling a faery, murder, and magic.

By

Melissa Marr

AVAILABLE now!

Chapter One

Autumn in the South was still both humid and hot. New Orleans was always a wet city. Wet air. Wet drizzle. Beer soaked streets. *Other* things spilling out from behind trash bins. Sometimes, the heavy air and frequent rain was just this side of too much.

Most nights, there was nowhere else I'd rather be. We were a city risen from the ashes, over and over. Plagues, floods, monsters. New Orleans didn't stop, didn't give up, and I was proud of that. Tonight, though, I watched the fog roll out like a cheap film effect, and a good book in front of a warm fire sounded far better than work. The nonstop rain this month would wash away evidence of the things that happened in New Orleans' darkened corners, but I could prevent bloodshed. It was more or less what I did. Sometimes, I spilled a bit of blood, but if we weighed it all out, I was fairly sure I was one of the good guys.

More curves and sass than actual *guys*, but the point held. White hat. Dingy around the edges. I blame my persistent nagging guilt.

A *thump* on the other side of the wall made me pause.

Could I hurl myself over the wall into Cypress Grove Cemetery? It wasn't the *worst* idea ever—or even this month —which said more about my life than I'd like to admit.

I listened for more sounds. *Nothing*. No scrabbling. No growling.

I needed to be on the other side of the wall where tombs were lined up like miniature houses. The tree branches I'd used last time were gone, probably trimmed by someone who saw their potential. Now, there was no graceful way to hurl myself over the ten-foot wall.

Every cemetery in the nation now had taller walls and plenty of newly-opened space for the dead. Cemeteries had become "stage one" of the verification of death process. Honestly, I guess graves were better than cold storage at the morgue. The lack of heartbeat made it impossible to know if the corpses would walk-again, and those of us who advocated for beheading all corpses were deemed callous.

I wasn't sure I was callous for wanting the dead to stay dead. I knew what they were capable of before the world at large did.

At least I was prepared. A moment or so later, I shoved a metal spike into the wall, cutting my palm in the process.

"Shit. Damn. Monkey balls."

A ripple of light flashed around me the moment my

blood dripped to the soil. At least the light was magic, not the police or a tourist with a camera. While the laws were ever-changing, B&E was still illegal. And I was breaking into a cemetery where I might need to carry out a contracted beheading. *That* was illegal, too.

It simply wasn't a photo-ready moment—although with my long dyed-blue hair and nearly translucent skin, I was far too photogenic. I won't say I look like I've been drained of both blood and color, but I will admit that next to a lot of the folks in my city, I look like I've been bleached.

I fumbled with my gloves, trapping my blood inside the thick leather before I resumed shoving climbing cams into gaps in the wall. Normally, cams held the ropes that climbers use. Tonight, they'd be like tiny foot supports. If I were human, this wouldn't work out well.

I'm not.

Mostly, I'd say I am a witch, but that is the polite truth. I am more like witch-with-hard-to-explain-extras. That smidge of blood I'd spilled was enough to send out "wakey, wakey" messages to whatever corpses were listening, but the last time I'd had to bleed for them to rest again, I'd needed to shed more than a cup of blood.

I concentrated on not sending out a second magic flare and continued to insert the cams.

Rest. Stay. I felt silly thinking messages to the dead, but better silly than planning for excess bleeding.

At least this job *should* be an easy one. My task was to find out if Alice Navarro was again-walking or if she was securely in her vault. I hoped for the latter. Most people hired me to ease their dearly departed back in the "departed" category, but the Navarro family was the other sort. They missed her, and sometimes grief makes people do things that are on the wrong side of rational.

My pistol had tranquilizer rounds tonight. If Navarro was awake, I'd need to tranq her. If she wasn't, I could call it a night—unless there were other again-walkers. That's where the beheading came in. Straight-forward. Despite the cold and wet, I still hoped for the best. All things considered, I really was an optimist at heart.

At the top of the wall, I swung my leg over the stylish spikes cemented there and dropped into the wet grass. I was braced for it, but when I landed, it wasn't dew or rain that made me land on my ass.

An older man, judging by the tufts of grey hair on the bloodied body, in a security guard uniform had bled out on the ground. Something--most likely an again-walker--had gnawed on the security guard's face. Who had made the decision to have a living man with no special skills stand inside the walls of a cemetery? Now, he was dead.

I whispered a quick prayer before surveying my surroundings. Once I located the *draugr*, I could call in the location of the dead man. First, though, I had to find the face-gnawer who killed him. Since my magic was erratic, I didn't want to send a voluntary pulse out to find my prey. That would wake the truly dead, and there were plenty of them here to wake.

Several rows into the cemetery, I found Alice Navarro's undisturbed grave. No upheaval. No turned soil. Mrs. Navarro was well and truly dead. My clients had their answer —but now, I had a mystery. Which cemetery resident had killed the security guard?

A sound drew my attention. A thin hooded figure, masked like they were off to an early carnival party, stared back at me. They didn't move like they were dead. Too slow. Too human. And *draugar* weren't big on masks.

"Hey!" My voice seemed too loud. "You. What are you . . ."

The figure ran, and several other voices suddenly rang out. Young voices. Teens inside the cemetery.

"Shit cookies!" I ran after the masked person. Who in the name of all reason would be in among the graves at night? I ran through the rows of graves, looking for evidence of waking as I went.

"Bitch!"

The masked figure was climbing over the wall with a ladder, the chain sort you use in home fire-emergencies. Two teens tried to grab the person. One kid was kneeling, hand gripping his shoulder in obvious pain.

And there, several feet away, was Marie and Edward Chevalier's grave. The soil was disturbed, as if a pack of excited dogs had been digging. The person in the mask was not the dead one in the nearby grave. There *was* a recently dead *draugr*.

And kids.

I glanced back at the teens.

A masked stranger, a dead security guard, a *draugr*, and kids. This was a terrible combination.

The masked person dropped something and pulled a gun. The kids backed away quickly, and the masked person glanced at me before scrambling the rest of the way over the wall—all while awkwardly holding a gun.

"Are you okay?" I asked the kids, even as my gaze was scanning for the *draugr*.

"She stabbed Gerry," the girl said, pointing at the kid on the ground.

The tallest of the teens grabbed the thing the intruder dropped and held it up. A syringe.

"She?" I asked.

"Lady chest," the tall one explained. "When I ran into her, I felt her—"

"Got it." I nodded, glad the intruder with the needle was gone, but a quick glance at the stone by the disturbed grave told me that a fresh body had been planted there two days ago. That was the likely cause of the security guard's missing face. I read the dates on the stone: Edward was not yet dead. Marie was.

I was seeking Marie Chevalier.

"Marie?" I whispered loudly as the kids talked among themselves. The last thing I needed right now was a *draugr* arriving to gnaw on the three dumb kids. "Oh, Miss Marie? Where are you?"

Marie wouldn't answer, even if she had been a polite Southern lady. *Draugr* were like big infants for the first decade and change: they ate, yelled, and stumbled around.

"There's a real one?" the girl asked.

I glanced at the kids. I was calling out a thing that would *eat* them if they had been alone with it, and they seemed excited. Best case was a drooling open-mouthed lurch in my direction. Worst case was they all died.

"Go home," I said.

Instead they trailed behind me as I walked around, looking for Marie. I passed by the front gate—which was now standing wide open.

"Did you do that?" The lock had been removed. The pieces were on the ground. Cut through. Marie was not in the cemetery.

Shaking heads. "No, man. The ladder the bitch used was ours."

Intruder. With a needle. Possibly also the person who left the gate open? Had someone wanted Marie Chevalier released? Or was that a coincidence? Either way, a face-gnawer was loose somewhere in the city, one of the who-knows-how-many *draugar* that hid here or in the nearby suburbs or small towns.

I pushed the gates closed and called it in to the police. "Broken gate at Cypress Grove. Cut in pieces."

"Miss Crowe," the woman on dispatch replied. "Are you injured?"

"No. The *lock* was cut. Bunch of kids here." I shot them a look. "Said it wasn't them."

"I will send a car," she said. A longer than normal pause. "Why are *you* there, Miss Crowe?"

I smothered a sigh. It complicated my life that so many of the cops recognized me, that dispatch did, that the ER folks at the hospital did. It wasn't like New Orleans was *that* small.

"Do you log my number?" I asked. "Or is it my voice?"

Another sigh. Another pause. She ignored my questions. "Details?"

"I was checking on a grave here. It's intact, but the ceme-tery gate's busted," I explained.

"I noted that," she said mildly. "Are the kids alive?"

"Yeah. A person in a mask tried to inject one of them, and a guard inside is missing a lot of his face. No *draugr* here now, but the grave of Marie and Edward Chevalier is broken out. I'm guessing it was her that killed the guard."

The calm tone was gone. "There's a car about two blocks away. You and the children—"

"I'm good." I interrupted. "Marie's long gone, I guess. I'll be sure the kids are secure, but—"

"Miss Crowe! You don't know if she's still there or nearby. You need to be relocated to safety, too."

"Honest to Pete, you all need to worry a lot less about me," I said.

She made a noise that reminded me of my mother. Mama Lauren could fit a whole lecture in one of those "uh-huh" noises of hers. The woman on dispatch tonight came near to matching my mother.

"Someone *cut* the lock," I told dispatch. "What we need to know is why. And who. And if there are other opened cemeteries." I paused. "And who tried to inject the kid."

I looked at them. They were in a small huddle. One of them dropped and stomped the needle. I winced. That was going to make investigating a lot harder.

Not my problem, I reminded myself. I was a hired killer, not a cop, not a detective, not a nanny.

"Kid probably ought to get a tox screen and tetanus shot," I muttered.

Dispatch made an agreeing noise, and said, "Please try not to 'find' more trouble tonight, Miss Crowe."

I made no promises.

When I disconnected, I looked at the kids. "Gerry, right?"

The kid in the middle nodded. White boy. Looking almost as pale as me currently. I was guessing he was terrified.

"Let me see your arm."

He pulled his shirt off. It looked like the skin was torn.

"Do not scream," I said. My eyes shifted into larger versions of a snake's eyes. I knew what it looked like, and maybe a part of me was okay with letting them see because nobody would believe them if they did tell. They were kids, and while a lot had changed in the world, people still doubted kids when they talked.

More practically, though, as my eyes changed I could see in a way humans couldn't.

Green. Glowing like a cheap neon light. The syringe had venom. *Draugr* venom. It wasn't inside the skin. The syringe was either jammed or the kid jerked away.

"Water?"

One of the kids pulled a bottle from his bag, and I washed the wound. "Don't touch the fucking syringe." I pointed at it. "Who stomped on it? Hold your boot up."

I rinsed that, too. Venom wasn't the sort of thing anyone wanted on their skin unless they wanted acid-burn.

"Venom," I said. "That was venom in the needle. You could've died. And"—I pointed behind me—"there was a *draugr* here. Guy got his face chewed off."

They were listening, seeming to at least. I wasn't their family, though. I was a blue-haired woman with some weapons and weird eyes. The best I could do was hand them over to the police and hope they weren't stupid enough to end up in danger again tomorrow.

New Orleans had more than Marie hiding in the shadows. *Draugr* were fast, strong, and difficult to kill. If not for their need to feed on the living like mindless beasts the first few decades after resurrection, I might accept them as the next evolutionary step. But I wasn't a fan of anything—mindless or sentient—that stole blood and life.

Marie might have been an angel in life, but right now she was a killer.

In my city.

If I found the person or people who decided to release Marie—or the woman with the syringe--I'd call the police. I tried to avoid killing the living. But if I found Marie, or others like her, I wasn't calling dispatch. When it came to venomous killers, I tended to be more of a behead first, ask later kind of woman.

Available May 2022
Pre-Order Now
The Fanged & The Fae: A Faery Bargains Collection

Three novellas in a book length collection:

"Blood Martinis & Mistletoe" (Set after book 1)

Half-dead witch Geneviève Crowe makes her living beheading the dead--and spends her free time trying not to get too attached to her business partner, Eli Stonecroft, a faery prince in self-imposed exile in New Orleans.

A walking-dead relative and a deadly but well-paying job make the holidays a lot more complicated than anyone needs. With a killer at her throat and a blood martini in her hand, Geneviève accepts what seems like a straight-forward faery bargain. Eli's terms might make the holidays a little more bearable, but if she can't figure out a way to escape this faery bargain, she'll be planning a wedding soon.

"Daquiris & Daggers" (Set after book 2)

A fun spa weekend away with friends in a city free of

monsters, what could be better? Gen's necromancy had been on the fritz, so a recharge sounds perfect—until she arrives in San Diego to discover that either the spa is too steps beyond weird or there's magic afoot

"Champagne & Commitments" (Set right before book 3)

Half-dead witch Geneviève Crowe makes her living beheading the dead--and trying to make sense of accidentally ending up a faery princess when she ended up bonded to Eli Stonecroft, a faery prince in self-imposed exile in New Orleans. But bonded for eternity isn't enough for family and friends--of her future citizens. It's time to plan a wedding ceremony. Unfortunately there isn't enough champagne available to deal with an undead-great-grandmother, a faery king who's trying to romance Gen's assistant, and a city where Halloween is a holiday worth dying to enjoy.

Available Fall 2022
Pre-Order Now
The Hexed & The Hunted: Faery Bargains

The third novel in a new faery and fanged world written by the author of the internationally bestselling Wicked Lovely series.

Half-dead witch Geneviève Crowe makes her living beheading the dead--and trying to juggle her new duties as a faery princess now that she's married Eli Stonecroft, a faery prince who was in self-imposed exile in New Orleans.

But monsters have no patience with royal obligations, and the same creature who once hunted her great-times-great grandmother is now trying to put Gen in the ground. When the relentless monster from her family's past decides to hex Geneviève, she's forced to go on the run or expose how much power she's started amassing. Her royally impatient uncle-in-law, the faery king, has already threatened her *and* Eli.

Death or Flight? Hexed or Hunted? This is *not* the honeymoon Gen and Eli were planning .

Melissa Marr is a former university literature instructor who writes fiction for adults, teens, and children. Her books have been translated into twenty-eight languages and have been bestsellers internationally (Germany, France, Sweden, Australia, et. al.) as well as domestically. She is best known for the Wicked Lovely series for teens, *Graveminder* for adults, and *Bunny Roo, I Love You* for young readers. In her free time, she practices teaches at an M.F.A. programs, mediates by way of medieval swordfighting, kayaking, and photography. Currently, she raises kids and chickens in the Arizona desert.

Visit her online:
http://www.melissamarrbooks.com